Never Rest

Jon Richter

This book is for Ashley, who waited for me on our path,
while I was lost in the wilderness.

Prologue

*he House of Madness
(first published in 'Real Life Horror Stories' issue 273 1
December 2002)*

There is a place, an island to be precise, that few people have visited, or even heard of. It sits in the Bristol Channel, a short boat ride off the north coast of Devon. Salvation is a cheerful seaside resort, boasting a windswept promenade, quaint gift shops, and friendly – if eccentric – locals. The island has many mysteries, the most famous of which is its abundant population of wild rabbits; lacking any natural predators and with dogs banned from its shores, Salvation is overrun by the inquisitive creatures, many of which are brave enough to eat right out of your hand. These quirks make the place an ideal outing for UK residents wishing to delight their young children, or to simply relax at a fraction of the cost of an overseas holiday.

But, before you consider paying the island a visit, please ensure you are first in possession of all the facts. Because, beneath its veneer of dated charm, Salvation has a dark and murky past. Poison gas testing, a WWII massacre, and UFO sightings are some of the site's mysteries, which we will explore in future issues. In this article, we will deal instead with Salvation's darkest secret of all: the appalling murders committed by the ferryman, Leonard Spitt.

If you ever travelled to the island between 1975 and 1996, there is a good chance that you were transported in Spitt's boat. Standing at 6'11", the boatman was an imposing figure, yet his almost childlike demeanour and booming laugh made him popular with visiting families. People called him Lenny for short, partly in homage to his namesake, another famous 'gentle giant'.

Little did they know that after nightfall, Spitt was using the craft for an altogether different purpose. Gripped by an unexplained and sadistic compulsion, he journeyed alone to the mainland, carrying with him a bottle of chloroform and some cloth rags. Here he would observe people taking a late-night stroll along the beach, perhaps walking their dogs. His victims were invariably young women, out strolling by themselves; their ages varied, but all of them were pretty, blonde and slim. Each one was seized, overpowered, knocked unconscious, and tossed onto his ferry like a piece of luggage.

Who knows how many others were considered for the same fate before Spitt selected his targets? How many were ultimately discarded in favour of some other, easier prey, unwittingly evading a brutal and violent death? We will never know, because Spitt is not alive to explain his actions to us. What we do know is that six missing persons cases were solved in 1996 when he walked into the local police station to confess to his crimes, and their bodies were found in his humble terraced house on Smalley Lane.

Fiona Prudence, Ella Wright, Gabby Kowalcyzk, Kate Byrne, Carol Schofield and Alice Goldsmith were identified, although the state of the remains means that police will never be 100% certain that more victims were not involved. Several of the women had been dismembered, their body parts used to create grotesque trophies and decorations throughout Spitt's house of horrors, with the remainder of their corpses dissolving to sludge in large acid barrels in the basement. In other instances, Spitt had used embalming fluid to preserve parts of the bodies, arranging them in obscene displays like shop-front mannequins.

One of the victims – tragically the youngest at only fifteen – had been flayed and nailed to the living room wall in the manner of an upside-down crucifix. Two others had had limbs removed and then stitched to each other's torsos, seated facing each other in chairs in an empty upstairs bedroom. Mercifully, these violations seem to have been committed post mortem, with a slit throat being Spitt's preferred killing method.

Other items recovered from the house included bowls made from skulls, from which Spitt had been eating; a necklace made from extracted teeth; various bones carved into tools and cooking utensils, many showing signs of use; and items of clothing made from skin that had been removed and dried.

What compelled Spitt to commit these atrocities? His suicide in his prison cell means we will never truly understand his madness. The last insight we have into his delusions is the words he scrawled in his own blood on the wall of the cell, having successfully sliced his own throat and wrists with a broken toothbrush. The gruesome message reads almost like a final, cruel joke from a truly twisted mind.

THIS VESSEL IS SPENT

There is little comfort to be taken from a tale like this. Perhaps the best we can do is surmise that, if Hell does exist, Leonard Spitt is certain to be burning in it.

Ian Skelton

SALVATION ISLAND

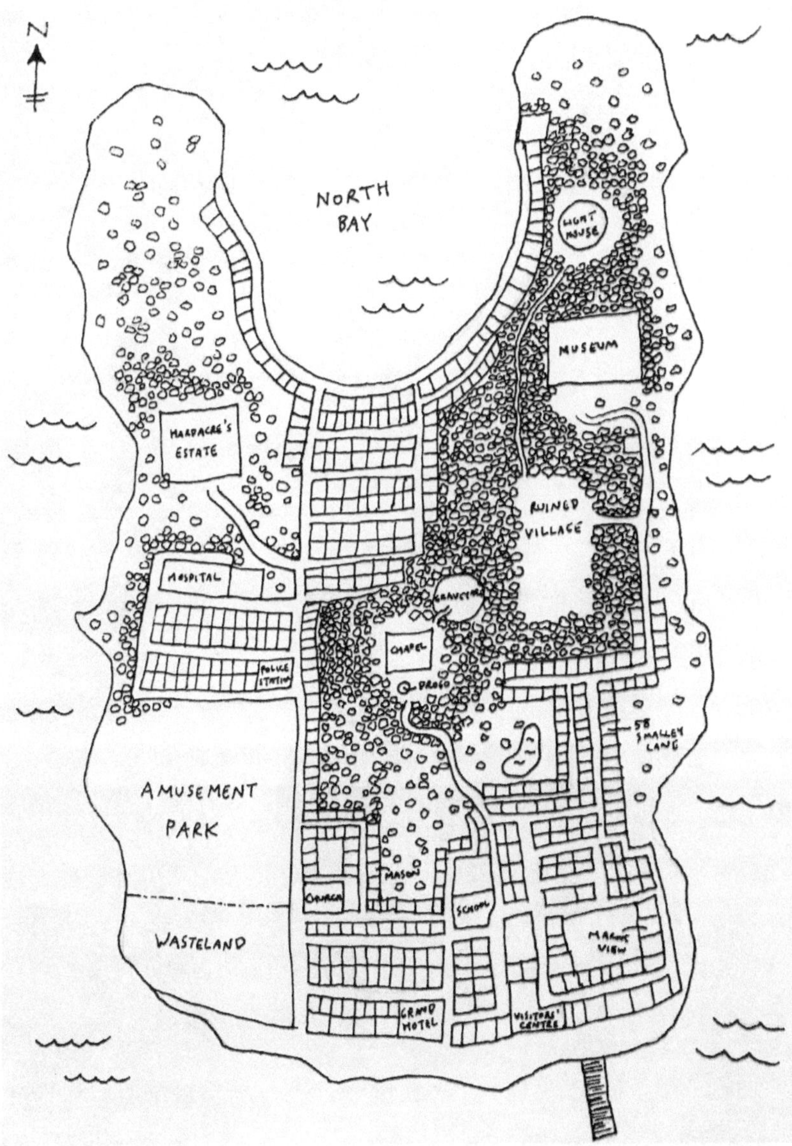

One (London)

He re-read the card and smiled, placing it carefully in the corner of his desk, at neat right angles to the hole punch and stapler: a thank you note from Diane Scargill, now calling herself by her maiden name, Diane Rathbone. He had provided her with proof of her husband's affair, and although the process of trailing the man had been sordid – snapping photos of him entering hotels with a young woman in dark glasses – perhaps this outcome made it worthwhile.

Perhaps.

He was used to this sort of sleaze, of course; after five years as a private eye, he was positively immersed in it. And he was good. *Sigurdsson Investigative Services* had earned him enough money to recruit an assistant, and he was hoping to soon be able to afford to move the two of them out of the oppressive crush of his cupboard-like office in central London. Nothing ostentatious, but at least something that he could keep *tidier*. A part of his brain still raged when he glanced across at Priya's workspace, wondering how someone so meticulously presented could work like such a slob.

"Are you going to moan about my mess again, Sigs?" she asked without looking up from her screen.

"Why ever would you think that?" he replied, making a point of wiping the dust from the pristine surface of his own desk. "Anyway, I'm fairly sure some of those old food containers are going to sprout legs and tidy *themselves* away soon."

"Ha!" she guffawed through a mouthful of Chinese, whose container was destined to become another mouldering carcass amongst the culinary graveyard that surrounded her laptop. "It's your fault for always making us work late, you slave driver."

"If you ever want to send a formal complaint, pass it over here in writing… or better yet, cut out the middle man." He gestured towards the wastepaper basket beneath his desk.

She laughed again, and he winced at the spray of sauce that emerged. "Even your bin is tidy, you weirdo."

He knew that she wasn't lying about the late nights. But he also knew that they weren't undertaken grudgingly, or at his behest; they were undertaken because Priya Chadha was conscientious, hardworking, and dedicated. And she was getting results.

In fact, she was a lot like someone else he had worked with, several years earlier. He found his thoughts drifting once again to DI Carin Mason. He had always meant to call her again, to stay in touch, to see if their relationship might blossom into… something else, once he had gotten himself sorted, got his new career off the ground. But after a while, it had seemed like too much time had elapsed. He had begun to doubt that he had anything to say to her, outside of the bizarre experiences they had shared, when they solved a strange case together. Gradually, months had become years, and the memories of Mason and Salvation Island had faded into a surreal, almost dreamlike memory.

And besides, she hadn't called him either.

"So how are you doing on the restaurant thing?" he asked Priya, trying to force his mind onto a different subject.

Mercifully, this time she swallowed her latest mouthful before answering. "It's difficult, because if their suspicions are true, the White Hart has already achieved its goal: the FSA shut the client down after the tip-off, when they found the rat infestation. So there's no way to catch the White Hart in the act, no reason for them to have kept anything incriminating. *But…*" Here her chestnut-coloured eyes gleamed excitedly, making her look even younger than her thirty years. "I managed to find a paper trail showing that the local pet shop sold eight rats recently to a Maria Jeffers, apparently a present for her daughter – and who is Maria Jeffers? Only the wife of the White Hart's landlord!" Priya sat back smugly. "Next job is to scope out their house to see whether they do indeed have any pet rats living there... or even any children."

"That's good work, Priya. But don't take it too far. Once you've checked out the lead, hand the evidence over to the client, and it's up to them what they do with it. Always remember–"

"I know, I know," she interrupted, rolling her eyes. "'Never do any more than the scope of our engagement.'"

He smiled. "That's the spirit. Soon you too can be a washed-up old gumshoe like me."

"What an honour... I suppose I've already got the failed police career to match." This was true. Like him, Priya was an ex-police officer. In her case, eight years of working the tough streets of East London had taken its toll, and she had decided to try something different.

"Touché," he responded, grinning as he packed away his laptop. "Seriously, don't work too late. I'm heading home now. Got to feed Casper. Then I'm going to try to figure out which cases we can take next, and which we'll have to turn down. It's a nice problem to have, I suppose."

"You know me, I've got nothing better to do, so I might be here a while yet. I'll lock up and everything. See you bright and early tomorrow, boss."

As he strode towards the door, he took one final glance around the cramped office, his case files, his talented assistant. His little empire. A small, proud smile formed on his lips. He had to admit that things were going well.

Then he thought of his tiny apartment. He thought of his advancing years, his fortieth birthday recently behind him. He thought about the long, lonely evening ahead of him, and his smile faded, just a little.

Two (London)

Casper eyed him disinterestedly from behind a rock as the food scattered across the water's surface. Sigurdsson wondered if his pet was sulking because he hadn't included any freeze-dried bloodworms, which were the fighting fish's favourite.

"What's the point of a special treat if I give them to you all the time, eh?" Sigurdsson chided as he replaced the tank's lid. He watched as Casper drifted languidly towards the floating pellets, gaudy frills twitching an alien dance of excitement. The fish consumed the food gradually, and Sigurdsson watched the strange movement of its jaws as it chewed and swallowed, regurgitated, and devoured again. Its scales sparkled in the reflected light, red turning gradually to blue along the length of Casper's body, making it look as if it belonged on another planet altogether, or in a dream. And yet here it was, in Sigurdsson's apartment, separated from him only by the walls of the tank.

Two solitary creatures, eking out their friendless lives on either side of the glass.

"I've only got you to talk to, haven't I?" Sigurdsson murmured, feeling an odd compulsion to reach into the water and stroke his pet's skin. "There's always Priya, I suppose, but outside of work it's just you and me, pal."

Casper swam a small figure-of-eight, which Sigurdsson decided to interpret as meaning 'yep… but that's not so bad, is it?', and he smiled as he started his stretches. He was planning a 10k run before he settled down to his evening meal, and to work through the casebook. He wasn't exactly a talented cook, but he'd been making an effort lately, and was quite looking forward to reheating the chilli he'd prepared over the weekend.

The sound of his phone vibrating on the glass surface of the coffee table startled him, and he hurried over to answer the call. An unknown number. Probably a recorded message telling him he was entitled to make a PPI claim or some such rubbish. But Casper seemed to be frowning admonition at him, and the run could wait a few minutes. He slid his thumb across the 'accept' symbol.

"This is Sigurdsson."

"Oh, hello. I'm sorry to call you so late."

"Who is this?"

"Erm, my name is Erina Brennan." The voice was a woman's, nervous and young sounding.

"How can I help you, Miss Brennan?"

"Actually it's… God. 'Miss'. That sounds so strange. I was about to say, 'it's Mrs'. But it isn't, is it? I mean, it *was*. I'm sorry, I'm babbling… let me start again. The problem is my husband… my estranged husband, actually. He's missing. I was hoping that you could–"

"Can I first ask how you got this number?"

"Oh, yes, of course. Someone gave it to me; in fact, they recommended you."

"I see. I don't usually give out this number for business calls."

"Oh, right. I'm really sorry. I knew I should have called earlier. I just don't really know how all this works…"

"It's okay, don't worry. What I would normally do is suggest we meet face to face to discuss the details of a case, and the fees. The problem is that we have a very full casebook already, Erina – do you mind if I call you Erina?" She told him that was fine. "Let me take down some details first."

He padded across the laminate floor towards the little kitchen area where a notepad rested on the breakfast bar. His voice echoed slightly as he spoke, as though reflected by the apartment's immaculate white surfaces. Casper's eyes followed him, perhaps wondering if he was going to fetch the tub of bloodworms from the freezer. "So your name is Erina Brennan?"

"Yes, that's right. Still technically Erina Lithgow, I suppose. I don't mind."

"And your estranged husband?"

"David. David Lithgow."

"How long have you been separated?"

"Just three months. It's been… a difficult year."

Sigurdsson recorded the details on the top sheet of paper as they spoke, the letters crisp and precise.

"So he was living separately from you prior to his disappearance?"

"Yes."

"And what's your address?"

"Um, I live at 36 Herron Way, in Bristol."

"Ah. I'm sorry, Erina, but I'm only accepting cases in London right now."

"Oh… oh no. I didn't realise… I thought that…" The woman on the other end of the line sounded close to tears, and Sigurdsson felt a pang of sympathy.

"But maybe I can still point you towards some help," he added. "I presume you've been in touch with the police already?"

"Yes, of course. David and I were still speaking regularly, about his latest bloody crackpot idea. And then he suddenly stopped calling me. His phone's been switched off for over four weeks. You must think I sound paranoid… but I just know, okay? I *know* there's something wrong. So I called the police, and they searched this terrible place he's been living, and they said… they said they found evidence of a mental breakdown." She paused, taking a deep breath, seeming to struggle to maintain her composure. "They think he committed suicide, and that's that. They're dredging the bay to look for his body. It's so awful…" Her voice cracked, and she fell silent.

"Was your husband being treated for any mental illness?"

Erina sniffed. "He was diagnosed as bipolar three years ago. You have no idea what it's like, Mr Sigurdsson. Unless you've lived with someone with that condition yourself, in which case you have my sympathy. He was so creative, so gentle… but he could be very unpredictable too."

Sigurdsson tried to steer her back onto the specifics. "So, the Bristol police – presumably they're treating this as a missing persons case?"

"Oh, no, sorry, it wasn't the Bristol police I spoke with. He doesn't live in Bristol. He's writing a book… He starts these projects and never bloody finishes them… It's about this island, and he went to live there while he wrote it, after we decided to separate for a while. I thought it would be good for him to focus on his work, give us some time apart to sort things out…" She sobbed once, a single anguished sound that seemed to tear itself up and out of her chest.

Sigurdsson didn't reply at first. He was too busy replaying her words, the pen clattering on the table top as it slipped from his hand. "This… island. Was it someone there who recommended me?"

"Yes. It was the policewoman herself, actually; the inspector, or whatever you call her. She said she understood my position but all she could do was keep searching for a body. She was very cold and matter-of-fact. I didn't like her one bit."

He remembered Mason's brusque demeanour, her constant stream of casual swearing. He remembered her apricot-coloured hair, her hazel eyes. "And your husband's book… was he writing about Salvation Island?"

"Yes. We used to holiday there together every year. I think he saw the place as a sort of… refuge. Somewhere to hide from all his pain, you know? I'm sorry to have wasted your time. Is there anything you can do? I feel so helpless… I know, I just know, in my heart, that he didn't kill himself."

A thousand fractured images seemed to flit before Sigurdsson's eyes, each one a tiny fragment of a five-year-old memory, like shards of a broken mirror.

Or droplets of blood, or light reflected in the eyes of a killer

"Erina, would you be able to meet me tomorrow afternoon?"

Three (Bristol)

Priya had been very understanding about his change of plan. In fact, she had seemed to relish the prospect of looking after the agency for a couple of days while he gallivanted off to the southwest. She'd even agreed to feed Casper for him while he was away, and he wondered what she would make of his spotlessly clean home. He imagined the state his apartment and the office might be in when he returned and shuddered; some things were too awful to even consider.

He was travelling to Bristol by train, as he'd long ago got rid of his car – it wasn't practical or cost effective to own one in central London – and so Erina had agreed to meet him at a coffee shop close to Temple Meads railway station. He'd thought about making the return journey that evening, but in the end, he'd checked into one of the budget hotels close to the station. He'd tried to convince himself that it was because the long round trip wasn't worth making in a single day… but if he was honest, he was secretly hoping that he might need to head straight onwards to the island. He'd even packed extra clothes, just in case.

He frowned at the thought, his emotions tangling around the memories of Salvation Island like strands of seaweed around a wrecked ship. He had nearly died there, a madman trying to hack him to pieces in his sleep, another madman trying to inject him with deadly poison. He had solved a murder case there, a series of events that had sucked him into its insanity and spat him out a changed man, cured of the crippling anxiety attacks that had plagued his adult life. He had met someone special there. Someone he still cared about. And she had apparently recommended him… was it simply a professional courtesy, or did it mean she still cared, too?

But this wasn't about Sigurdsson. This was about a troubled, missing man, and his poor wife, who despite their separation wanted desperately to find him. This was about Erina Brennan, who perhaps wanted to remain Mrs Erina Lithgow. Sigurdsson glanced around the coffee shop, sipping his latte while he searched for a woman who matched the description she'd given him.

Dark glasses and dark hair held up in a red headscarf. That was her. He took his coffee over to the table. "Erina?"

She lowered her own cup from her lips as he approached, leaving a crimson stain on its edge. The scarlet hue of her lipstick and headgear accentuated the paleness of her skin, making her appear almost spectral. "Yes, that's me. So, you're… Mr Sigurdsson?" She stood to shake his hand, her grip weak and cold, as though her recent stresses had drained her of all fortitude.

"Yes, but please call me Chris. Thank you for meeting me here."

"Oh, that's okay. I work nearby anyway."

"What do you do?" he asked as he sat down.

"I work in publishing. That's how we met, you see. David sent in a manuscript, and I loved it. I ended up becoming his editor for a while. He was so endearingly neurotic. A typical writer."

"How long were you married?" She looked as young as she had sounded on the phone, surely no older than thirty, and had presumably started work at the publishing company after leaving university. This meant that their marriage had lasted perhaps six years. It was something he'd started to do almost by default – making assumptions and educated guesses about people, then finding ways to test them.

"It would have been six years this November," she replied. "He was very open with me, about his illness. I suppose maybe I thought it was part of the package… the whole 'troubled writer' thing. I was young, and naïve… I thought I could 'fix' him."

She hadn't taken off her glasses, but Sigurdsson could tell that her gaze had drifted off towards the window, outside of which a pleasant summer day was coasting into the past tense.

"And you haven't heard from him?" he asked gently.

"No. His phone's still off, and the police haven't found anything."

"Okay. Here's what I suggest. I know she can be a bit... insensitive, but I once worked with DI Mason, and she was an excellent detective."

She hadn't actually been a detective at the time – that was part of the reason he'd been deployed to assist her, although that was probably more to do with the sexist machinations of their former superior officer – but it had been no surprise to Sigurdsson when she'd passed the exam a few months later.

"I've been meaning to visit her on the island for a long time, so this is a great opportunity for me to finally do it," he continued. "I'll travel there at no charge and speak with her about David's disappearance. If I think I can do anything to help you, I'll give you my quote. If I honestly think I'd be wasting your money, I'll tell you, and leave the case in her capable hands. Does that sound okay?"

Partially hidden behind the dark glasses, Erina's expression seemed to be one of surprise, and immense gratitude. She sounded close to tears as she replied. "Oh, Detective... Chris... thank you! Thank you so much. I just know that you'll find him... wherever he's gone."

"I will do my best, Erina. I promise. Now I need you to tell me some things about your husband. Is this the first time he's ever disappeared?"

She shook her head firmly. "No. I suppose this was part of it... how our marriage broke down. I once got home from work to find a note telling me he 'needed some space' and that he would call me in a week's time. In the end he rang me three nights later from some cabin in Scotland, saying he was really sorry, that he knew he'd been an idiot, that he wanted to come home if I'd have him back. Then he did the same thing again a year later, only this time it was five days until I heard from him."

"Was this… part of his writing process, somehow?"

To Sigurdsson's surprise, she laughed. "What writing process? After the first book, he didn't write at all. We lived off my salary while he complained about his writer's block, his creative inertia, whatever his excuse was that month for not actually doing anything."

"I see. That must have been difficult."

"It was. I knew what I was getting myself into… or I thought I did. I was going to be this wonderful, supportive person… his 'rock'. He was going to be a bestselling author. And now look what's happened to us."

Her head dropped in resignation. She was still wearing her wedding ring. Sigurdsson decided not to pry too much into the details of their marriage. Better to concentrate on getting a feel for David Lithgow as a person, the specifics of his illness.

"Is David receiving any treatment for his disorder?"

She shook her head.

"No… he got the diagnosis years before we met, and he said at first he tried CBT and anti-depressants, but they all just made him feel like he was trying to 'suppress himself'. I thought he had come to terms with who he was, found a way to cope."

"But he might have started treatment again since you separated?"

She shrugged sadly. "We still talk a lot but… yes, I suppose he might have, and not told me. But I think it's unlikely."

"How long have you been separated?"

"Three months. God, I can't believe it's already been that long."

"And has he been on the island all that time?"

"Yes."

"How old is David?"

"Is… you keep saying 'is'. The policewoman said 'was'."

"I'm sure she doesn't mean to upset you."

"He's forty-one. Ten years older than me. He doesn't look it though," she added, then bit her lip, seemingly embarrassed at the irrelevant detail.

"How tall is he?"

"Six feet two." She answered straight away, without hesitation. Details she was very familiar with. A person she cared about, had built her life around.

"Can you email me a photograph of David, if I give you some details?"

"Yes, of course. In fact, I've got one here. You can take it. It only makes me sad when I look at it."

"I'll be sure to return it," Sigurdsson replied as she handed him the small picture from her purse. It depicted her standing next to a tall man with a wild, curly mop of hair, and a gaudy scarf that made him look like Tom Baker in *Doctor Who*. She was looking at him with real laughter in her face, and without the glasses, Sigurdsson could see that she was very pretty. David Lithgow was staring into the camera, pulling a silly face. They looked like a nice couple.

"I'd rather you just return *him*," she replied despondently.

Sigurdsson didn't know what to say, so he said nothing as he slipped the picture into his own wallet, swapping it for a business card which he handed to her. She took it and studied both sides; one bore his contact details, the other the company logo he'd come up with: *Sigurdsson Investigative Services* written above a staring eye, the text curved to fit the stylised oval shape. Beneath the eye was the slogan 'We Never Rest'.

"It's based on the logo of the Pinkerton Agency," he told her. "Have you heard of them?"

"No, I'm sorry."

"They were the first real detective agency. They started in the US in the late 1850s, founded by a Scottish immigrant called Allan Pinkerton. At one point, they were so successful that they allegedly had more operatives than the entire US army at the time. Their logo, which I've shamelessly ripped off, inspired the term 'private eye'."

"And you've based yourself on them because you're really good at your job?"

The note of forlorn hope in her voice was so tragic that Sigurdsson couldn't bring himself to respond with his customary modesty. "Yes, I'm good at my job. I will find out what's happened to your husband."

She smiled and thanked him, while he winced internally at the promise he'd made.

Four (Bristol)

Sigurdsson sat on the corner of his bed in the hotel room, his phone pressed against his ear. He still had Mason's number (he'd tidied up his contact list several times over the last few years but had never been able to bring himself to delete it) and had checked it with Erina in case it was out of date. It hadn't changed. He wondered if Mason herself had; if the island was as he'd left it, the crumbling, melancholic shadow of a seaside resort.

And now he was actually calling her. He remembered feeling like a lovesick schoolboy at times when he last worked with her, and now here he was again, a middle-aged man in a hotel room, sweating and breathless because of a childish crush on a professional colleague.

The call went to voicemail. He didn't know whether to be devastated or relieved. A warm, queasy feeling unfurled in his stomach as he listened to her speak.

"This is Carin Mason. Leave a message after the beep and I'll get back to you as soon as I can."

It beeped.

"Err, hello. Hi, Carin."

He panicked and ended the call.

For God's sake, Chris! He decided to take some time to calm down before calling her again, so he unfolded the battered ironing board he'd borrowed from reception and set about readying a shirt for the following day.

The phone vibrated in his pocket. It was Mason.

He took a deep breath, remembering the anxiety attacks that used to plague him, and then answered, as nonchalantly as he could.

"Um, hi."

"'Um, hi?' What's that supposed to mean? Your voicemail wasn't any more bloody eloquent either."

He smiled. "Yeah, err, sorry about that, I think I got cut off. It's Chris, Chris Sigurdsson."

"I know who it is. I wondered if Lithgow's wife would contact you."

"I should thank you for the recommendation."

"Yes, well, I suppose it was a bit selfishly motivated." His heart leapt. So she *had* wanted to see him? "I had to get rid of her somehow – the poor woman had been crying in my office for an hour." His heart deflated like a pierced balloon.

"I see… so you fobbed her off with my details?"

"No, no, I didn't mean that. Look, Chris; there's no case to solve here, except for where and how he killed himself. The guy was a complete nutcase."

"I think the technical term is 'bipolar' these days, Carin," he replied frostily.

"You need to come and see where he was staying. What he wrote."

"You mean his book?"

"She told you about that, did she?"

"Only that it was about the island's history."

"That isn't the half of it. Do you remember me telling you about Leonard Spitt?"

More fragments of memory. Mason, slurring her words as she chatted to him in a bar, poking him in the chest to emphasise her point.

"Wasn't he a serial killer, before your time on the island?"

"That's right. Six women murdered and mutilated. An absolute fucking monster. Lithgow was writing a book about him."

"Okay. I imagine it isn't the most pleasant read."

She laughed harshly. "Chris, he moved into Spitt's *house*. Where all the bodies were found. Lithgow was fucking *living there*."

He blinked, shocked. "Jesus," he murmured eventually.

"More like the opposite, I'd say. Anyway, if he was trying to get into Spitt's mindset, it seems to have worked. There are reams of nonsense all over the house, Chris. Typed pages and scribbled notes stuck on the walls. Drawings. Pagan symbols. Gibberish. The bloke was having a full-on breakdown. It's like the whole house is one great big cryptic suicide note."

Sigurdsson frowned. "Has his wife seen it?"

"Yep. I thought it might get it across to her that her husband was really in a bad place, help her move on. But I don't think she'll accept it until I find the body. And that's proving a tad difficult at the moment. I've already dredged the bay; you remember, where we eventually found Vic Valiant?"

As she mentioned their previous case, he searched her voice for something, some echo of affection, some longing for his company. But there was nothing. Mason was cold and business-like. Just like when they had first met.

"I remember. But there are plenty of other ways he could have done it. For all we know he might even have left the island."

"Exactly my point, Chris."

He sighed. "I made her a promise, Carin. I said I'd go and take a look and let her know if I thought there was anything I could do to help. Free of charge, at least at first."

"That's very noble of you. Well, be my guest. I'm short-staffed as it is. Giggs took a job in Ilfracombe and I wasn't allowed to get a replacement – budget cuts and all that – so it's just me, Mitchell and Clive these days."

"Okay. I'll get the ferry across tomorrow morning. She gave me the address, but she didn't mention about it being… the murder house."

"She probably thought you'd share my point of view. I don't think she likes me very much."

"If you are right, and he took his own life, hopefully I can at least help you find him." He paused, bit back the words he was about to say. *And it'll be good to see you.*

There was a sudden, urgent beeping sound from the other side of the room. He glanced across to see smoke billowing from beneath the iron. "Bollocks!" he yelped as he dived across the bed to switch off the device. By the time he picked up his phone again, Mason had hung up. A text message from her read, simply:

See you tomorrow. I'll be there at eleven.

He sighed. He hadn't even had a chance to ask about Holly, her daughter, who would be about ten by now. And Mason had seemed distant, perhaps even annoyed with him.

Or perhaps she was simply being professional. He had to remember that she probably hadn't thought about him once for the past five years.

He picked up the shirt and stared through the blackened, iron-shaped hole that had been burned through it, right where his heart would have been.

Five (The island)

Sigurdsson had slept badly, probably because he'd stayed up late reading about Leonard Spitt online. The man really had been a monster, and in more than one sense: physically he had been a giant, standing almost seven feet tall. Such was his immense size, he even sometimes appeared as a performer in the island's 'freak show', which was apparently still running. But Spitt's main job had been to ferry passengers between Salvation and the mainland, in the direct employ of Thomas Hardacre, the island's owner (now succeeded by his son, Edward, following Thomas's death in 1997). Spitt had been a popular character, thought of as something of a loveable simpleton.

There hadn't even been an active murder investigation when he'd handed himself in; just a slew of missing persons cases that hadn't yet been connected with the island. But then Spitt had confessed to the crimes, and the police had broken into his house, and the officers must have thought they'd stepped straight into a nightmare.

Now Sigurdsson sat on the passenger ferry, his destination that same ghoulish house. It was probably the same boat he'd ridden on his last journey to the island; and in another parallel with his previous visit, there were very few others travelling with him, despite it being mid-June, approaching holiday season. Salvation's popularity as a tourist attraction clearly continued to diminish. He closed his eyes, remembering how the island had emerged suddenly from the fog, like a sea monster. At least there should be clearer skies this time.

But once again, as they approached, the place seemed to be shrouded in mist, as though obscured by a sinister enchantment. Slowly its menacing silhouette swam into view: a hill covered in twisted trees; a distant lighthouse; a Ferris wheel that never ran. The island gave the impression that its form was transient, like a malign presence that hovered just behind the swirling brume, manifesting itself physically only when it chose to.

As they drew nearer, he saw that the seafront was busier than the last time he had visited, but not by much. Given that they were approaching the start of summer, he'd expected a bustle of visiting tourists wandering between the chippies, amusement arcades and gift shops. But instead, most of the outlets were closed, some even boarded up. The few people that he could see seemed to be alone, shuffling along the promenade with their heads bowed as if in mourning for their dead island, while seagulls circled above them like vultures.

The rabbits, of course, were still present. Despite the chill of the mist, groups of the creatures were visible all along the promenade, picking at piles of discarded food. Sigurdsson liked rabbits, but these did not resemble the cute and inquisitive animals he was familiar with: they looked desperate, their bodies gaunt, their eyes wide and feral. *More like giant rats than bunnies*, he thought with a shudder. He hurried past them, their disconcerting stares following him as he headed towards his hotel.

He was staying at a bed and breakfast called the Marine View. A stooped, elderly man named Doug welcomed him, explaining that he was the sole proprietor and insisting on carrying Sigurdsson's small suitcase up the stairs, despite his protestations. As they ascended, the old man asked about his reason for visiting.

"Just here to see an old friend," Sigurdsson replied, and Doug seemed content with that, and didn't ask him anything else.

Sigurdsson couldn't get any decent roaming internet connection on the island, but the Marine View had free Wi-Fi, so he looked up the route to Spitt's house online and scribbled a map on a piece of paper. It wasn't far. He suddenly had a vivid flash of memory: Mason, driving them in her squad car, her voice sarcastic as she told him that, on Salvation, nothing was far away.

The island's layout was fairly straightforward: behind the south-facing promenade and its row of rundown bars and shops were a few residential streets, before the housing gave way to the rising swell of the central hill and the forest that clung to it. At the top of the hill were the chapel and the cemetery, and the statue of Saint Drogo that had brought the island some fame in the 1950s after a spate of 'miracle healings'. (Sigurdsson remembered his visit to the strange monument, when he had rubbed its famous bronze foot and made a wish, lashed by the pouring rain.)

A theme park occupied the island's southwest corner, and the residential area behind it continued past the hill's west side, curving round to the north where it connected to another collection of tourist outlets that encircled the bay. To the east was the lighthouse, close to the former convalescent home that had been rebuilt after its obliteration in a World War II bombing raid, and now operated as a museum. South of that was a ruined village that had been preserved as a sombre tourist outpost, and then the clockwise circuit was completed by more housing that re-joined the promenade's east end.

Only a few square miles, and home to fewer than two thousand people. Was one of them David Lithgow? Or had the writer – in one sense, or another – already departed?

Spitt's house was towards the east side of Salvation. The island was silent as Sigurdsson headed towards it; no cars on the roads, no people walking past. The contrast with London was stark and should have given him some welcome respite from the chaotic grind of the city. But somehow, Salvation's stillness did not seem peaceful; it was as if the island had detected the presence of an outsider and coiled in on itself like a serpent.

Sigurdsson reached Smalley Lane at 10:56, and found that Mason was early. She was leaning against the front wall of number 58, looking at her phone, and glanced up as he approached.

That same hot feeling in his gut. Her hair was longer, curling slightly around her shoulders, still the same kumquat colour. Her figure was slim, not tall but not petite, athletic but shapely.

"Hi, Carin."

"Hello."

He smiled, and she did too, but hers seemed forced somehow, and he again wondered if she was angry with him.

"Are you ready for your grisly ghost tour?" she quipped.

"I suppose so," he replied, and she immediately turned to walk through the gate and up a short path towards the nondescript, white front door. Had he expected a few pleasantries, even an inquiry about what he was up to these days, besides being a private eye? For all she knew he might have gotten married since they last met. Then again, for all he knew, she might be in a relationship too. Maybe that was why she was being so formal with him.

She unlocked the door and stepped inside. He followed her, pausing at the threshold as a strange and momentary feeling of dread overwhelmed him. He wondered what it must have been like for the police officers who entered the house back in 1996; had they even truly believed the claims Spitt had made in the police station? Even if they had, nothing could have prepared them for the atrocities that awaited them behind that innocuous front door.

Sigurdsson swallowed the feeling, burying it in the same place he'd buried his anxiety attacks years earlier, and stepped into a tiny hallway that contained a pair of doors, one ahead and one to the left. A smell immediately reached him: an oppressive, thick odour suggesting human occupation and a lack of regular cleaning.

"That one leads to the basement," Mason said, gesturing to the door ahead of them. "There isn't much to see down there. But if you go through into the front room, you'll understand what I'm saying about Lithgow."

She pushed open the left-hand door. Instead of a chamber of horrors, a scene of maniacal creativity confronted them.

Every surface was plastered with David Lithgow's outpourings. The walls were covered with pages of notes, sketches, handwritten scribbles and printed photographs, almost obscuring the peeling wallpaper beneath. Many of the pages had further stickers and Post-its attached to them, and Sigurdsson's eyes were drawn to the disturbing questions they bore:

Why here?

Only entrance?

Not enough bodies?

The surprisingly large living room contained a dining table, but this was almost hidden beneath a pile of further writing; an old printer was barely visible beneath the heap, which spilled onto the carpet and around the legs of the only chair. Sigurdsson could see hand-drawn maps, diagrams of some sort of ritual, and hundreds of pages of typeface. An attempt had been made to tidy some of the papers on the floor, but the stacks of A4 had quickly become precarious towers, transforming the journey from one side of the room to the other into a bizarre obstacle course.

The room's 'centrepiece', occupying the space opposite the tattered couch where you might have expected a television set to be, was a makeshift poster comprising about sixteen sheets of paper that had been fixed scruffily together with Sellotape. It bore the haunting legend:

This place is a nexus, a convergence of realities —
I am a vehicle for the will of other worlds

"I remember that," Sigurdsson murmured, still taken aback by the chaotic scene. "You told me that quote once. It's what Spitt said to your predecessor, after he was arrested."

"That's right. It always stuck with me. I'll admit that I was pretty freaked out when I saw it written there."

"Is there anything else?"

"Only more of this. It goes all the way into the kitchen, up the stairs, into the bedrooms… it's like he turned the whole house into a giant scrapbook."

"What happens to all of this? I mean, if he was only renting the place, presumably the owner will want it cleared out?"

"The house belongs to Edward Hardacre. He owns the whole island; a lot of the residents rent their places from him. He used to be worth a fortune, but I'm not sure now with the island going to shit. Anyway, I met with him and managed to convince him to give me a fortnight. If I don't find the body by then, he wants to put a new tenant in here, and we'll have to remove all of Lithgow's… work."

"So how much time have we got left?"

"Less than a week."

Sigurdsson nodded, then grimaced. "Seems a bit wrong somehow, renting out a house that six people were once found murdered in. Shouldn't it have been demolished or something?"

Mason shrugged. "No law says it has to be. Hardacre can rent it out as long as he can find people willing to live here. Maybe it's cut-price rent though." She surveyed the room's outlandish décor. "Or maybe there are plenty of weirdos willing to pay a premium."

Sigurdsson didn't reply, carefully negotiating the piles of paper as he continued to explore the house. Like Mason had said, the notes and images continued throughout its interior. They were pinned to the front of cupboards in the kitchen, attached via magnets to the fridge, stuck on the wall alongside the staircase. Some of the pages looked like copies of photographs of the house as it was when the police first raided it, and he wondered where Lithgow had obtained the images. Sigurdsson saw gruesome ornaments made from bones, bodies arranged in disturbing tableaus… and perhaps most ominously, a series of pictures of large blue barrels.

"You said there's nothing in the basement?" he asked.

"Yeah, it's empty. Not even any of his writing down there. Maybe he just hadn't run out of room in the house yet."

Or maybe spending time down there was too unnerving a prospect, thought Sigurdsson.

Mason followed him upstairs, where the house contained a bathroom and three bedrooms.

"It looks like he was sleeping in this one." She gestured towards the smallest room. "Interestingly it's the only one where he hasn't stuck anything on the walls."

"Maybe he needed somewhere he could retreat to, when he'd had enough of… his thoughts."

"Maybe. There are loads of clothes still in the drawers and wardrobe. His laptop was left downstairs, and his suitcase is under the bed… it doesn't seem to me like he left here on a trip."

"Was his passport left here too?" Sigurdsson asked.

"Yep. Even his wallet. The only thing that's missing is his phone."

"Was there anything on the laptop?"

"Nope. It was almost like he'd deliberately wiped it, before he left for the last time."

"Hmm," Sigurdsson murmured, peering inside the wardrobe at a drab array of dark outfits. "So what's your theory? You're saying he killed himself – but why, and how? And where?"

Mason frowned at him, then seemed to soften. "Look, I know everyone thinks I'm a cold bitch, and I'm not pretending to be a psychiatrist. But he was clearly a man with… problems. Agreed?"

Sigurdsson nodded. "This doesn't feel like a manic genius at work. I agree with you that this looks like someone having a breakdown."

"I think he was obsessed. I think he got too wrapped up in his project. His marriage had fallen apart, and he was trying to forget about it by concentrating on this book. But it was all going wrong. He couldn't keep track of all the information. Or maybe he was searching for a conspiracy that wasn't there, seeing patterns where there weren't any."

She opened the door to another bedroom, where more of Lithgow's frenzied scrawling was plastered across the walls. Here, pages representing ideas or clues were linked by coloured string stretched between pins to form a kind of 3D 'mind map'. 'Fiona Prudence' was linked by blue strands to 'Croyde Bay' and also to 'runaway' and 'slit throat', which in turn was joined by a purple thread to three other women's names. There were dozens of these connections, some of which had further notes dangling from them, giving the impression of a kind of kaleidoscopic spider's web. The room was virtually impenetrable as a result.

Mason closed the door. "I think it gradually all became too much for him, and one day he snapped, and decided to commit suicide. His wife said he'd tried it before. Whether he jumped into the bay or went somewhere to hang himself, I don't know. We've interviewed everyone that has operated a ferry since his disappearance, and no one remembers seeing him... but that doesn't prove that he didn't leave the island to do it."

"Without his wallet?"

She shrugged again. "I agree, that does make it more likely that he stayed here on Salvation. But maybe he wasn't thinking straight. Maybe he only took cash with him."

"Have you found any drugs in the house, any medication?"

"Nothing. He didn't even have any booze here. Hardly any food either, for that matter."

Sigurdsson wandered into the largest bedroom, where another banner greeted him. This one bore another strange phrase.

This vessel is spent

"Any idea what *that* means?" he asked.

"Not a clue."

"There's just... so much *information* here. It's a lot to take in."

"Or a load of nonsense not worth wasting your time on."

"Is that really what you think? That it isn't even worth trying?"

Mason's face hardened. "Look, if you want to pore over every last word of this, be my guest. I've got other things to do, you know, besides trying to decipher the ramblings of a crazy man."

"Carin, I didn't mean it like that."

"No, it's fine. Here, I'll even let you keep the key – I've got spares at the station."

She tossed the key at him and turned to walk out of the room.

"Carin, wait!" he shouted after her as she descended the stairs.

"Forget it, Chris. I'm just… you must remember the joys of working with me. I'll speak to you tomorrow. Let me know if you decide to stick around."

And with that, she closed the front door behind her, and left him alone with David Lithgow's thoughts.

Six (The island)

Sigurdsson spent the next hour trying to devise a methodical approach to reading all of the house's material, but he couldn't concentrate. Maybe it was the place itself – the spectres that seemed to dance among the dust motes, to crawl across the pages of Lithgow's handiwork – or maybe Sigurdsson was distracted by his frustration with Mason. Why was she behaving so strangely? Hadn't she more or less invited him here in the first place?

He decided he needed to clear his head. As he stepped outside and locked the door behind him, he was quickly reminded of the island's stubborn resistance to the season; an icy chill hung in the air, and the mist meant he could barely see beyond the end of the street. He drew his thin jacket about him and walked briskly, heading in no particular direction, until he reached a scattering of trees that marked the outer edge of the forest.

The last time he had been here, the trees had been bare, their gnarled branches reaching upwards like grasping talons. Now they were covered in leaves, but they somehow looked no more alive; the foliage was streaked with a sickly, greyish rot, as though the island was stricken by some internal disease. This whole place – the trees, the rabbits, the residents – seemed blighted. Accursed.

He entered the forest and felt the gradual increase of the incline, leading him upwards towards Drogo and his chapel. He tried not to think about the pairs of eyes regarding him from the undergrowth: the rabbits, breeding and dying, breeding and dying. The woods had to be riddled with their corpses.

He focused instead on the matters at hand. Did he really think he could help Brennan find her husband? He couldn't help but agree with Mason: what Lithgow had done to the house suggested a fractured mind, a man on the edge of a crisis. But did that really mean they should just abandon the poor couple? Surely Brennan deserved, at least, some closure... he hated that word, but throughout his career, he'd learned that people really did seem to benefit from knowing the truth about their loved one's fate, however tragic. If David Lithgow had committed suicide, if his body was hidden somewhere on the island, his estranged wife deserved to know. She deserved a chance to move on with her life.

But what did he really expect to find? Mason was a good policewoman. She had searched the obvious places. To charge Brennan a hefty fee and then deliver no results would be worse than a professional failure; it would be immoral.

As he walked on, and the wretched trees closed in around him, he decided to call her.

She answered almost instantly. "Oh, hello, Mr Sigurdsson... Chris. Have you been to the island?"

"Yes, I'm there now. I've been to the house. You didn't tell me about... David's work."

"I'm sorry," she replied eventually. "I thought you might... I didn't want you to write him off as a loony."

"I understand. And psychiatry is certainly not my field. But I do think you need to at least consider the possibility that David was having difficulties."

Silence again. Then a firmer, more resolute tone.

"Do you know what it's like, living with someone with bipolar disorder?"

"No, I don't," replied Sigurdsson honestly.

"The last time we spoke... he sounded so focused, so energised. He said 'I'm onto something, Erina. It's really big. This place... it's not what it seems.' I thought perhaps the separation was working for him, helping him concentrate on his writing. It made me sad and happy at the same time. But I know…" She paused for a moment before continuing, drawing a deep and fragile breath. "I know that the next day he might have woken up in despair, thinking everything was hopeless again. But he wouldn't just… he would have called me…" Once again, her words faltered, her voice cracking. It must have torn her apart, thought Sigurdsson, having to flit between the roles of supportive partner, adoring wife, thick-skinned carer. He waited for a few moments while she composed herself, then spoke.

"Erina… the truth is I don't know. I don't know if Mason's right, and there's nothing more I can do to help. But I want to try. So, here's what we'll do. Give me three days. If I find nothing, and make no progress, I'll write it off as a…" He glanced at the gloomy, oppressive vegetation that surrounded him, "…as a holiday. But if I can find out what happened to your husband, I'll charge you a flat fee of two thousand pounds. No extra charges, VAT already included. Does that sound reasonable?"

"Yes. Yes, that sounds perfect. Thank you, Chris."

"Okay. I'll call you with a progress report the day after tomorrow."

She began to say something but stopped. Then she said it anyway. "I started reading it, you know. The pages on the walls, all over the floor. I thought I'd be able to piece it together; that it would all make sense to me, because I know him so well. That I'd find out where he went and be able to save him." She sighed wretchedly. "But it's all just… gibberish. I know he needs help. I know that. I can't bear the thought of him hanging from a rope somewhere, with no one there to comfort him, no one to talk him out of it, to tell him how much we all love him…"

Sigurdsson thought she might break down into tears again, but she didn't. "I will do everything I can, Erina. I promise."

"Thank you," she said again, and hung up.

He exhaled deeply, feeling drained after the exchange. The poor woman. But she had said something interesting, something that continued to resonate in his mind as he navigated his way back through the silent forest towards the house that had once belonged to a killer.

I'm onto something, Erina
It's really big
This place… it's not what it seems

Buried somewhere in the morass of words and images that adorned its walls, the house might contain a clue to David Lithgow's whereabouts.

Seven (The house)

Sigurdsson decided to start in the basement and work his way up.

Pushing open the door that led down to the underground chamber, he felt the same wave of fleeting terror that he'd experienced when he first stepped into the house itself. He was gripped by the irrational idea that somehow the mutilated bodies were *still down there*; that he'd peer down the stairs to see dead women hauling themselves out of their blue barrels, crawling towards him, dragging strips of dissolved skin behind them along the floor.

But, like Mason had said, there was nothing down there. He flicked on the light at the top of a narrow, wooden staircase, which led him downwards between two walls – he couldn't help thinking of the visible brickwork as the house's exposed insides – before stepping out into a large, empty room with a surprisingly high ceiling. *Spitt must have enjoyed the space in which to work*, Sigurdsson thought grimly as he stared at the tarpaulin covering the floor, imagining dark bloodstains beneath. But whatever other paraphernalia Spitt had kept down here had long since been removed, and David Lithgow had not replaced it with anything of his own. No bicycle, no old tools, no broken TV set. Only some visible pipework, and an aura of lingering horror that was almost palpable.

Sigurdsson didn't want to spend another moment down there and had to will himself not to break into a run as he climbed the stairs and slammed the door on the loathsome space.

The living room and its bizarre decoration was positively comforting in comparison. Sigurdsson decided to start to the immediate left of the door he had just passed through and work his way clockwise around the room.

The first document he looked at was a printout of a newspaper article.

Local ferryman commits suicide in custody after confessing to horrific crimes

The worst nightmares of the families of a number of missing women were tragically realised this week when their bodies were discovered inside a house on Salvation Island. Disturbingly, the house's owner, Leonard Spitt, had operated the ferry from the mainland to the island for over twenty years, and was a familiar face to holidaymakers and locals alike. Neighbours have been shocked by the discovery of the remains of Fiona Prudence, Ella Wright, Gabby Kowalcyzk, Kate Byrne, Carol Schofield and Alice Goldsmith, which were found mutilated and partially dissolved in acid in the basement of the house on Smalley Lane.

"Lenny always seemed a little peculiar, but no one thought he was capable of this," said one appalled resident, while another told us, "He was such a nice man. Children on the island used to call his name when they saw him, and he'd always smile and wave back."

The island recovered from near-destruction during the Second World War to become a successful holiday destination, although its popularity has declined in recent years, leading to the closure of many of its attractions. Now its beleaguered community will have to adjust to another blow: that of becoming forever associated with a series of brutal and sadistic killings.

Spitt, who confessed to the murders in police custody, has since committed suicide in his cell, denying the victims' families the chance to see him brought to justice for his crimes.

The next page was a strange, typed essay that seemed to bear no relation to Spitt.

The black heart

It beats at the centre of our world, behind the eyes of every desperate vagrant, every malicious child, every greedy executive. It's the bond we all share, the terrible kinship of mortality: a morbid fascination with death, with suffering, with cruelty.

Is it any wonder that all of our most famous stories involve conflict, bereavement, and pain?

We award Pulitzer Prizes to suicidal photographers who are glorified by suicidal songwriters who are idolised by suicidal teenagers.

We feast on the bloody misery of our past and tell ourselves that it's in the name of progress, of making things better.

Beat/

Rain beats down on the mud of Auschwitz, and dead fingers claw their way up from the muck, corpses disgorged from the earth as if the ground itself is sickened by our crimes

Beat/

A starving child covered in its own shit cries for its mother, who lies dead in the arms of her junkie boyfriend in the next room

Beat/

Eyelids are cut away to prevent torture victims from hiding from the devastation of their bodies

Beat/

I wanted to write something truly grotesque. A scathing commentary on the human condition; a brutal, dystopian, compellingly repulsive piece of decadent gothic art.

But it's all been done, already. Humans have been writing it since we first crawled out of the swamp.

The eccentric ramblings continued, each page seemingly bearing no relation to the next; a collection of thoughts, musings, excerpts, and quotes acting as a physical manifestation of the turmoil of Lithgow's mind.

'Then Jesus said unto them Verily, verily I say to you, Except ye eat the flesh of the Son of man, and drink his blood, ye have no life in you. Whoso eateth my flesh, and drinketh my blood, hath eternal life: and I will raise him up at the last day. For my flesh is meat indeed, and

my blood is drink indeed. He that eateth my flesh, and drinketh my blood, dwelleth in me, and I in him.'

Sigurdsson kept reading, transfixed, working his way upwards from the floor. He realised he would need to find a stepladder to be able to read the higher pages, such had been Lithgow's determination to cover every inch of the walls with his indecipherable work.

Alone

Lone	Hate	Torment	
Loner	Envy	Torture	
Tired		Violence	Hurt
		Worthless	
			Forget
			No days
			Death
			Repent
			Resent
Tired			
Sleep	Sleep	Sleep	Sleep
Sleep	Never		

Another shiver, a sensation like clammy hands at his throat; the memory of a different Chris Sigurdsson, one who was plagued by anxiety and fear; another page.

I learned a lot about Leonard Spitt when my wife and I went to Salvation for the third time. Visiting the island had become an annual ritual for us – we didn't have enough money to holiday overseas, and the place's quaint and faded charm seemed to appeal to both of us. She found it relaxing, while I found it inspired me to write.

We hadn't managed to visit the museum on either of our previous visits, so we made sure we took a walk to the island's north side to check it out this time. The air was cold as we walked there, like it always is. We held hands and it was so lovely Erina Erina Erina Erina Erina Erina Erina Erina Erina please comeback to me

The curator was a peculiar man, but very charismatic. I got the impression they didn't have many visitors, and he was only too happy to show us around in person. His knowledge of the island was encyclopaedic, and some of the exhibits were impressive. But I was particularly struck by the story of Spitt; what could drive a man beloved by his community to commit such vile acts? He told me a lot about the case, and it must have triggered something in me, a story perhaps, the germ of an idea.

One of our favourite things to do was to take the walk up the hill to the chapel, to rub Drogo's foot and make a wish. It was our third visit, and we were making the climb once again, the air cold and refreshing, like it always is. We held hands and it was so

perfect Erina Erina Erina Erina Erina Erina Erina Erina please comeback please ple

This time we had a look around the little overgrown cemetery, and I spotted Spitt's name on one of the graves. It was jarring to imagine him buried there, his evil bones only a few feet beneath us. I suppose I'd always thought killers were burned to dust, thrown away, expunged from the world.

The museum curator had recommended more books I could read about the island's history and the Spitt murders in particular, and I started to devour them as soon as we arrived home.

Sigurdsson slumped into the couch, drained. This was an impossible task. It would take him more than three days to read the contents of this room alone, never mind the entire house. He needed a way to filter more quickly through the content, to pinpoint any information that might actually be relevant to Lithgow's disappearance.

He decided to start with the papers on the desk: he would reorder them, sort the daunting mass into piles by subject. "All right, David," Sigurdsson muttered as he sat down on the solitary chair. "You must be in here somewhere."

The sun's glow, blanched to a sickly pallor by the fog, slowly dwindled to darkness, like the guttering flame of a candle. Sigurdsson barely noticed. He ignored the fading light and the hunger pangs in his stomach, the missed call and voicemail from Priya. He concentrated on the task and didn't rise from the chair until he had created five neat piles: items seemingly unrelated to Salvation; miscellaneous sketches; articles or historical data about Salvation or Spitt; maps; and photographs. The first three were interesting but he had deemed them non-urgent – some of the sketches in particular looked like little more than absentminded doodles, although all were disconcerting in their content. The maps might be of more practical use, as some of them clearly depicted the island, and therefore maybe locations that Lithgow had visited. But many of them were perhaps historical records; certainly, the road network depicted bore little resemblance to the streets he had traversed during his time on the island.

The photographs were similarly difficult to interpret. Many contained buildings, or peculiar objects whose significance he could not fathom. One of them was a photograph of an altar, complete with a metal bowl and an ornamental knife. He also found pictures of each of Spitt's victims, six women who bore a striking resemblance to each other, their names written beneath printouts of their smiling faces. He hadn't yet found a photograph of their killer, although he did find what looked like a grainy CCTV image of a wide, bald man walking between buildings, with something slung over his shoulder. The man was looking almost directly into the camera, his features blurred but unmistakably smiling.

Finally, Sigurdsson had found one other note, very hastily scribbled, that defied his classification system, and so had merited the creation of a sixth pile, all by itself.

In Lithgow's feverish, jerking scrawl, the note contained four names, listed beneath a baffling heading.

POSSIBLE CULT MEMBERS

Marion Weisberg
Octopus Girl
Edward Hardacre
Donald Armitage

He had no idea what it meant, but it was his first tangible lead. And although he had no idea who Marion Weisberg was, or what 'Octopus Girl' meant, he did recognise the last two names. Edward Hardacre was the island's owner, and Donald Armitage had been Salvation's chief of police, before Mason had taken over from him following his retirement.

He returned Priya's call.

"Did you get my message?" she asked, once again sounding like she was talking through a mouthful of food. He realised that he hadn't eaten anything since breakfast.

"No, sorry. I haven't listened to it yet – is anything up?"

"It's fine now. I wanted to know how your stupid oven works, but I figured it out."

"Oh, okay, good... my oven?" He executed the verbal equivalent of a double take.

"I'm at your flat, aren't I? I thought I may as well have my tea here after feeding your fish – he's weird, by the way."

"He probably thinks the same about you," Sigurdsson retorted. "Did you give him a couple of bloodworms as well as the pellets?"

"Yeah, yeah, I remembered... Thanks for that disgusting task by the way. It's no wonder he lives alone."

"You're supposed to keep them by themselves. If I put another in there it would be carnage."

"Even a female?"

"Yep. You have to introduce them for just long enough to lay their eggs in the male's bubble nest, and then take them out again, otherwise the male will attack her."

"Uh-oh."

"What does *that* mean?"

"So I shouldn't have bought you another one from the pet shop as a surprise?"

"You did *what?*"

"He looked so lonely..."

"Priya! You need to get the other one out of there *right now!*"

"Relax, I'm kidding!" Her laughter roared down the phone. "Blimey, you think I'm completely stupid, don't you? Sometimes I wonder why you hired me. Then I remember: it's because I'm gorgeous, and talented."

Sigurdsson was unimpressed. "So, do you have any *important* updates to give me?"

There were a few seconds of chomping before Priya replied. "Nope."

"Right. In that case I need you to stop stuffing your face and do something for me. I need phone numbers for two people: one is Edward Hardacre, who owns Salvation Island. The other is Donald Armitage, the former DI."

"And you expect me to do that from here?"

"I know you. You're already working. Your laptop is open in front of you on my coffee table. Probably covered in bits of chow mein."

He heard Priya huffing, and then the sound of fingers rapidly tapping on a keyboard.

"I don't see why you couldn't just do this yourself," she muttered.

"I left my laptop at the B&B – I'm still at the murder house. The missing man turned it into a sort of… live-in diary."

"Hmph. Your case sounds more exciting than mine."

"I've given myself a three-day deadline to make a breakthrough, so don't get too comfortable in my flat."

"Three days of wild parties with Casper? Yippee!" He heard more typing. "Right, I've got the details for you. Armitage moved to Bristol. I've got a landline number for him. Hardacre is in Padstow, but he has a house on the island too. I've got the numbers for both. I'll text them all to you. Now bugger off while I finish my tea. And for your information it isn't Chinese this evening; it's a frozen curry from your freezer."

"I was saving that!" he hollered, but she had already hung up. Seconds later, the text came through. He smiled and tried the mainland number for Hardacre. His eyes roamed the walls as the phone hummed its dial tone, his expression twisting into a frown as his gaze fixed on some of the ominous words and phrases that surrounded him.

More victims

Trigger

Orphans

Inverted cross

Missing interview tape

What happened to Spitt's parents?

The phone continued to ring. Eventually Sigurdsson gave up, and instead tried the number for Hardacre's other home, on the island. Once again, it rang incessantly, not switching to voicemail, as though mocking him. He let the ringing continue as his gaze wandered towards the kitchen, to the back window beyond, the small rectangle offering a view of a modest back yard bathed in the day's fading, ruddy light. Sigurdsson knew that the garden had been dug up following Spitt's confession, and so the paving slabs must have been laid since then. He also knew that no further horrors had been found beneath the soil; Spitt's atrocities had been confined to the house's interior, the bodies denied even the small decency of a burial.

Photographs of blue barrels, designed for storing corrosive chemicals

He gave up on Hardacre. He dialled the number for Armitage, and the retired policeman answered on the second ring.

Eight (The house)

"Hello?"

"Please may I speak with Donald Armitage?"

"This is Donald. Who is this?"

"Mr Armitage, I apologise for using underhanded means to acquire your phone number." He might as well be honest. "But I'm hoping that when I explain my reasons, you will be willing to help me."

Silence at the other end. Sigurdsson continued hastily, not wanting to blow his opportunity. "I'm a private investigator, working on a case on Salvation Island."

"I'm retired. Talk to Carin Mason, if she's still there. She was my replacement." Armitage's voice was stern, but he didn't hang up. Perhaps the old man enjoyed being reminded of his younger days. Perhaps he lived alone, and the phone call was a welcome intrusion on another lonely evening.

"I have. She and I are... old associates. She recommended that I call you." A little white lie wouldn't hurt.

"What's this about, Mr...?"

"Sigurdsson. My name is Chris Sigurdsson. Chris is fine. I'm investigating a missing persons case. A writer living on the island has disappeared."

"I still don't understand why Mason thought I could help with this."

"The missing writer was writing a book about Leonard Spitt."

"Oh. I see." Three short syllables, but loaded with emotion, like a thousand dreadful images had slammed into Armitage's brain, all at once.

"DI Mason has hit a brick wall. The writer's wife has asked me to look into it. So, I'm trying to figure out the missing man's mindset, to learn the same things he had learned about the Spitt case. He thought he'd made a big breakthrough of some sort."

Armitage grunted. "I'm not sure how that could be. I wouldn't even call it a 'case'. Spitt murdered those girls right under our noses, and we all had no idea it was happening. Then he handed himself in, and then he committed suicide. I presume you know all the specifics?"

"Everything that's publicly available, yes."

"So you know what we found in that house."

"I know about the six victims, and what he did to their bodies."

"But still, you can't imagine it, Sigurdsson." Armitage's voice dropped almost to a whisper. "Even if you saw photographs of that place... actually *being* there was a thousand times worse. It was like we'd stepped into Hell."

He was silent for a few moments, and Sigurdsson waited patiently as the older man's mind transported him backwards, to somewhere very dark.

"I had a deputy with me," he continued, eventually. "He was only nineteen. He had to run straight outside to be sick. I was trying to be the strong, wise old hand, teach him what he'd have to get used to as a policeman. But not that. No one should get used to that."

Another long pause. "It was pure evil, what Spitt did. Not of this world. After five minutes in that house I was outside puking my guts up too." Armitage sucked in a long, ragged breath, as though trying to calm himself. "The oversized halfwit that lumbered into my police station that morning didn't seem capable of it. His confession was like... a recording. Like he was reading lines from a script. I didn't even believe him until I saw it myself." He fell silent.

"The man I'm searching for has been renting the house Spitt used to live in," Sigurdsson ventured. "Staying there while he worked on his book. Looking for... inspiration, I suppose."

Armitage didn't reply for a long time. Sigurdsson wondered if the old policeman had hung up, until he simply murmured, "good God," and then was silent again.

"I don't think he was in an entirely sound state of mind, prior to his disappearance," Sigurdsson continued. "But he was certainly working very hard. Your name appears in one of his notes. I take it he didn't contact you for an interview?"

"No. This is actually the first call I've had for months. My children have their own lives now, and my ex-wife couldn't care less. The divorce... sometimes I even blame that on Spitt. On what I saw in that terrible place. That bastard didn't just ruin the lives of his victims and their families. It was like that house poisoned everyone who entered it."

Sigurdsson felt a shudder shake his body. He realised that he had stood up and wandered upstairs while he talked and was now staring into the bathroom. Was that the same sink, into which Spitt had doubtless washed litres of blood? He decided not to advise Armitage of his current whereabouts.

"The missing man's name is David Lithgow. In one of his notes there's a quote, something I believe Spitt said to you; he talks about the island being a–"

"'This place is a nexus, a convergence of realities. I am a vehicle for the will of other worlds.' Is that the one?" Armitage's voice took on a haunted, broken aspect as he recited the words. Sigurdsson felt another shiver crawl through his bones.

"Yes, that's it. I'm sorry if I'm bringing back bad memories, Mr Armitage. But I wanted to know if there was any significance behind the quote, anything I'm missing."

"No. I never had a clue what he meant. It just... stuck with me, over the years. 'This place'... when he first said it, I thought he meant the island. But later I became convinced he meant *the house itself.*"

Sigurdsson headed back down the stairs, suddenly feeling breathless, the walls and David Lithgow's words seeming to slowly close in on him. "Was there... anything else?" he stammered as he descended. "About Spitt, I mean; anything else he said, that you think might be significant?"

Armitage seemed to answer a different question. "I felt responsible. For his death, I mean. I should have searched him more thoroughly, taken that bloody toothbrush off him. It was my fault he was never tried, never convicted or punished for what he did." The old policeman's voice hardened as he continued. "You say you're looking for a writer? I don't like writers. Some of those bastards over the years have said that Spitt was innocent, that we bullied the confession out of him, that he had mental health problems; that he was as much a victim as those poor girls."

Armitage was becoming more and more agitated. Sigurdsson felt suddenly guilty for telephoning this poor old man, making him relive a damaging experience. But all Sigurdsson could do now was listen; listen, while he stared at the picture he had found, a printed photograph stuck to the back of the kitchen door.

"Let me tell you something: that bastard knew *exactly* what he was doing."

Spitt's face grinned back at him, a wide smile beneath large, empty eyes. The face looked somehow inhuman – but not in a monstrous way. More like a rubber mask; a crude and unsophisticated approximation of a person's face, like a low-budget android in a sci-fi movie, with a vacant expression fixed hauntingly in place.

"He became like a bogeyman, after that," Armitage continued angrily. "He was a big fella, for sure, but suddenly all the kids on the island were saying he was ten feet tall, that he was immortal, that he lived in the woods and would break in and steal them from their beds at night. People were dressing up as him at Halloween, for God's sake. I was surrounded by these caricatures, these jokes… It was almost like the youngsters here had adopted him as some sort of mascot. But they didn't know… none of them could imagine what he was *really* like. Those glazed eyes, looking at you, looking through you; like he was in another place altogether, and you weren't really there. Not one shred of remorse for what he'd done."

Sigurdsson tore his eyes away from the dark void of Spitt's stare. He felt a swell of panic, rising and spreading; something he hadn't experienced for many years. "Mr Armitage," he began, not even sure what he was going to say, just wanting to regain control. "The missing man wrote something else. Something about a cult." *A cult that he seemed to think you were a member of.* "Do you know anything about that?"

Armitage surprised him by scoffing haughtily. "Oh, it's a load of rubbish. More kids' stuff. One minute we were a nice little seaside town, the next we were a bunch of devil worshippers, or cannibals. That cult was another stupid myth. If that was your man's big breakthrough then I'm afraid his book wasn't going to be much good."

"Can you remember any details about this supposed cult? Its name, its activities…?"

Armitage sighed, sounding suddenly drained. "Mr Sigurdsson, I've given you all the time I can manage. I need to go now. I've got… things to do." A real sadness permeated those last three syllables. Sigurdsson thought about pushing for more information, but he couldn't bring himself to distress the older man any further.

"Thank you, Mr Armitage, for your time. I hope I don't need to contact you again. In the meantime, might I leave you my details, in case you think of anything that might be relevant to the case?"

But the line was already dead. Everyone seemed to be hanging up on him lately.

He sagged into the couch, tilting his head back to stare up at the white expanse of the ceiling, finding solace in the absence of notes and pictures there. He closed his eyes and let a long breath escape from his lips, as though purging himself, as he tried to contemplate his next move. But all he could think about was that terrible expression: Spitt's facsimile smile, like a face made from wax.

"Sod it," he muttered eventually. "I need another break."

He set out into the night as though he was fleeing from something.

Nine (The island)

Sigurdsson wasn't dressed for jogging, but he ran anyway, his long strides carrying him rapidly along the desolate stretch of the seafront. He didn't know exactly why he had become such a keen runner. He liked the cadence of it, his body settling into a steady rhythm while his mind seemed to escape from its confines, released like steam drifting upwards into the air. Here he could gather his thoughts, reflect on the day, the case, his plans, his life; hovering above his physical body while it just ran, and ran, and ran.

He thought about Mason, who had asked for his help, but now seemed angry with him. Perhaps he should talk to her about it, cut through all the pleasantries and ask what he had done wrong. But he didn't want to drive her further away. He knew that a part of him was here for her, after all.

He thought about Erina Brennan. A part of him was here for her, too. He had made a commitment, however ill advised; she would be pinning her hopes on a positive update when he called her in two days' time, and so far, he hadn't made any progress. But he was sure that the answer was somewhere in that house, in the arcane labyrinth of Lithgow's writings.

He thought about Leonard Spitt. The man had been a conundrum, an enigmatic evil. To understand Lithgow's actions, he felt sure that he would have to follow the missing writer deeper into the killer's mind.

He thought about Salvation itself, wrapped in its cloak of mist and riddles. He remembered his last visit, the late-night jaunt that had led him to the chapel at its centre. To the strange effigy that watched over the island like the monarch of a forgotten kingdom.

Perhaps he would pay Saint Drogo another visit, rub the statue's magic foot again, make another wish; after all, at least in part, the last ones had come true.

He thought about his Marcus, his younger brother who had died in a tragic car accident aged only six, and the absence of pain made his heart feel simultaneously guilty and glad.

Rabbits scuttled out of his way into the darkness of a side street as his feet pounded past them. But he didn't follow them north, towards Drogo's hill. Instead he continued towards the southwest corner of the island, where the creatures had virtually overtaken the abandoned amusement park. He had begun to think of it as their 'home', and the rabbits he encountered elsewhere as brave foragers, or perhaps outcasts. He passed no one on the promenade, although one or two of the bars did appear to be open, snatches of music and conversation grasping at him as he jogged past.

After about half an hour, he had reached the chain-link fence that surrounded the derelict area. He had planned to simply get there and then turn and run back to the B&B, to get an early night and a fresh start the following day. Yet instead he lingered, drawn towards the forsaken place. It was dark, and he could see nothing beyond the fence; until a light flickered, a few hundred feet away. It darted this way and that, like a will o' the wisp.

Or the beam of a torch.

Why would someone be in the amusement park at this hour... or at all?

There was no reason for this to be remotely relevant to his investigation. It was probably a security guard, or some mischievous teenagers. But his curiosity compelled him to search for a way in, enticing him towards that mysterious light. It didn't take him long to find a gap between two fence panels, and he squeezed between them, cursing as he snagged his leg and tore his jeans.

On the other side of the fence was a barren patch of land, and Sigurdsson crept across it, crouching low to stay out of sight and to scour the ground for any rabbit holes in which he might twist an ankle. He made slow progress towards the light, which itself seemed to be moving gradually to his left, towards the western perimeter of the park, and the sea. He usually carried a torch with him, but he hadn't brought it along for his run, and even if he had, using it would only give away his position. He realised this meant that if the torch he was following was suddenly switched off, he would be stranded in absolute darkness. The thought of standing there, surrounded by countless scuttling rabbits, made his skin crawl.

He quickened his pace, and eventually reached a dilapidated wooden structure. The torch beam was barely twenty metres away, playing left and right as whoever wielded it made their way slowly westwards. He could see a row of similar buildings opposite, and realised that they were game stalls, huts that would once have housed coconut shies, shooting galleries, hook-a-duck challenges. The stalls, painted in gaudy colours that had long ago faded and peeled, formed a street between them, funnelling visitors onwards to the next attraction. Towering above him, invisible in the darkness, he sensed the looming spectre of the Ferris wheel.

He couldn't see anyone else illuminated by the torchlight. This was a solitary explorer, inexplicably wandering through the park's decaying remains.

Who would be out here alone in the middle of the night?

His mind conjured all manner of sinister explanations, to envisage a menagerie of monsters that might be gripping the other end of the torch. Searching for him.

The towering frame of Leonard Spitt himself, the island's sinister bogeyman

This was ridiculous. Sigurdsson was creeping around in the dark, following someone. For all he knew they had heard his footsteps and were terrified themselves. He called out just as the beam flicked to the right, but the suddenly-illuminated image of a giant grinning skull made the words stick in his throat, and all he emitted was a strangled grunt.

The light spun around, away from the ghost train, and dazzled him like the glare of an oncoming vehicle.

"Who's there?" called a woman's voice, sounding frightened but firm.

"I'm sorry," replied Sigurdsson, shielding his eyes from the torch beam. "I saw the light and thought… I don't know what I thought. What are you doing in here?"

"Oh dear," came the reply. "I'm not causing any trouble. I'll leave straight away. Please don't call the police."

Sigurdsson frowned, squinting to try to see the woman behind the dazzling light. "Why would I do that?"

"Aren't you… a security guard?"

"No, I'm a detective."

"A detective?" The woman's voice was a mixture of fear and confusion.

"I'm not here for you. I'm investigating a missing persons case. I just thought… I wanted to know why someone would be out here. Other than me, I mean."

"If you're a detective, show me some ID," she replied, unconvinced.

"If I do show you some, how will you know if it's even real?"

"I don't know… I don't know what else to ask for. I'm terrified that you're a flippin' rapist, alright?" Anger had entered her voice now.

"Okay, sorry, I understand. I'm sorry I sneaked up on you. Let's walk back to the seafront, together. I'll walk well in front of you, so you can keep the torch pointed at me. Then when I'm back on the other side of the fence, maybe we can talk? Here's my Private Investigator's Licence." He took out his wallet and produced the card.

She pointed the torch at it. "You're right – I haven't got a clue what that card is. It could be your Blockbuster Video membership for all I know. But I like your suggestion, so get walking. But just so you know, I'm an urban explorer, and I have a video camera strapped to me. So, I'm going to be filming everything you do. If you try anything funny, it'll be on tape."

He opened his mouth to point out that if he had wanted to attack her he could easily steal and destroy the camera afterwards, and then decided this probably wouldn't help the situation. So instead he turned and walked. She followed, ten metres behind, the torch pointed at his back as if he was marching at gunpoint.

"What did you say you were?" he called back over his shoulder. "An urban explorer? What's that?"

"I make films of old abandoned buildings. When I'm not being interrupted by creepy detectives, that is."

"You make documentaries?"

"Not really. This is just for fun. Although I do post all my stuff on YouTube."

"It sounds like a dangerous hobby," he replied, gingerly picking his way back across the waste ground towards the fence and the reassuring glow of the streetlamps.

"This place is nothing. I've been on my own in abandoned mental hospitals, underground bunkers, haunted castles… You should watch my videos." She seemed proud of her work.

"They sound too scary for me," he replied, wondering if he should simply make his apologies and leave her to her bizarre pastime. He reached the fence and began to search for the gap he'd entered through.

"Try here," she said, pointing the torch to his left. He spotted the gap, and squeezed once again between the segments of fencing, careful this time not to further damage his clothes.

"Thanks," he said, turning to face her. She kept the torch trained on him. "My name's Chris. Chris Sigurdsson. Like I said, I'm searching for a missing person. I can see you're not in any trouble, so I'll leave you in peace to carry on your… filming."

She pointed the torch towards herself, giving her face a spooky up-lit effect. She was about his age, maybe a little older, with dyed blonde hair pulled back into a ponytail.

"My name's Daisy," she said, her eyes narrowing. "I probably shouldn't trust you. But I've decided that I do. So, I'm going to come out there and talk to you."

She clicked off the torch and walked towards him, sliding gracefully out through the same aperture. Beneath the softer light of the streetlamp he could see that she was short, with a strong-looking, sturdy frame and a pleasant, freckly face. She was wearing an orange puffer jacket and a sort of multi-purpose utility harness that held water bottles, energy bars, a chest-mounted camera and what looked like some sort of grappling hook.

She extended a gloved hand to him.

"Chris, did you say?" He nodded, returning her handshake. "I was about to go into the ghost train. I thought it would be cool to make a video of me exploring a creepy theme park in the dark. Especially *here*," she emphasised, sweeping her arm to presumably indicate the entire island.

"What, is Salvation some sort of mecca for urban explorers?"

"More or less. And we call it 'urbex' by the way. I'm doing the ruins tomorrow and then the convalescent home, although that doesn't really count because they've converted it into a museum."

"I see."

"But you know about the island, right? UFO sightings, serial killers… This place has *everything*. I've been meaning to come here for months."

"You're brave to go in there by yourself. Or nuts. Old buildings can be dangerous, you know. It might collapse on you. Or there might be squatters in there. Or old syringes."

"Or toxic bat shit. Or rotten floorboards. Or creepy detectives following me in the dark. I can handle myself, thanks. I do take precautions, you know; I don't just blunder in wearing flip-flops."

"It still seems a strange thing for…" His voice trailed off.

"What? For a *woman* to be doing?" she challenged, glowering at him.

She had a point. Was it only her gender that was resulting in his patronising urge to protect her? And from what – a load of mouldy old ghost train dummies? And yet…

"Do me a favour, will you? I can't let you go back in there alone. And I know you won't want to take a 'creepy detective' in there with you."

"Sounds like you're too scared."

He scoffed theatrically. "No, I just don't have my… urbex gear with me, right now. Why don't you come for some food with me instead? My treat. One of the bars on the promenade. You can tell me all about this hobby of yours. And then you can come back tomorrow and do all the trespassing you want, when I'm not here."

She screwed up her face as she considered his offer. "Alright then. It *is* a bit later than I intended. And I've already got plenty of footage for today."

He smiled.

"Plus this has to be the weirdest date I've ever been on," she added, laughing.

"It's not a date!" he protested. "But I can't leave you out here alone with that giant skeleton."

"Yeah, yeah. You're the one who nearly screamed when they saw it. So where are we going? The Cloak and Dagger?"

"Why not?" he replied, thinking that it sounded very apt.

Ten (The island)

It turned out that Daisy was, to put it as kindly as he could, completely bonkers. The bar she had suggested was a pub that looked like it hadn't been refurbished in decades; the chairs and booths were all chipped wood and sagging red leather, the carpet a tattered collage of stains that might once have been burgundy. The place reeked of stale beer and cigarettes, and Sigurdsson could well believe that it hadn't been cleaned since the smoking ban was introduced. An assortment of pictures adorned the walls: old photographs of the pub and its various landlords, several caricatures of the same people, and slogans like *'Free air guitar with every pint'* and *'Alcohol: helping ugly people have sex since 1862'*.

After some bland burgers, Daisy had immediately insisted that they buy two rounds of rum and cokes, before launching into a protracted monologue about her childhood in Bolton, the greatest conquests in her six-month urban exploration career, the photography degree she had recently completed, and her three failed marriages.

"How long have you been on the island?" he interjected when she finally paused to glug her drink.

"A few days. I'm staying just up the road, so this pub's my local. It's cool, isn't it? Kind of shabby and smelly, exactly like…"

"An old shit pub?" he ventured, and she guffawed loudly, polishing off the drink in another swig.

"Anyway, I want to hear all about your detective work. It sounds *exciting*."

He knew he was wasting time. But it was nice to be out drinking with someone funny, who seemed to enjoy his company – or at least to find him a good listener. Maybe he simply needed a break from his thoughts, from that house…

"It's not quite like the movies, I'm afraid. But it can be interesting sometimes. It's rewarding to help people."

"You said you were searching for a missing person?"

"That's right. He was living here on the island. He was a writer. I don't suppose you've met him?"

He produced the photograph he'd obtained from Brennan. Daisy studied it, her tongue protruding between her lips as she concentrated.

"Nope, sorry. So, what's happened to him? Has he been abducted, or something?"

Sigurdsson carefully tucked the photograph back into his wallet. "I don't know. But my job is to find out."

"I could follow you around. Make a documentary of your investigation." Her eyes gleamed dangerously at the idea.

"Err… maybe concentrate on the theme park for now, Daisy. Right, I'm just going to nip to the Gents – I'll be back in a minute."

"I'll get the next round in!" she retorted and hurried off to the bar.

One more drink, he thought. *Make sure this lunatic gets home safely, then head back to the Marine View*. Then wake up the next day and figure out what the hell he was going to do next.

As he walked towards the toilets in the far corner of the bar, he noticed a pretty waitress collecting glasses from one of the other tables. She caught his eye and smiled at him.

Still got it, Chris, he thought as he pushed open the door to the WC, seconds before he smacked his head on the low doorway. The sharp, unexpected pain caused him to stumble backwards, his vision swimming.

When it cleared, the waitress was leaning over him. "Are you, all right? Do you want some ice?"

"I'm fine, I'm fine… just *really* embarrassed," he replied, cringing at the sound of a few locals chuckling nearby.

"There's a sign, you know. It says, 'mind your head'."

"I wish I'd read it," he replied, clambering to his feet. She extended a hand to help him up. Her other hand was hidden within the odd, long cardigan she was wearing, as if it might be injured and held in a sling.

"Thanks," he said, smiling sheepishly. "I'll try that again."

She really is pretty, he thought as he ducked into the toilets. There was something Eurasian in her weary, almond-shaped eyes and friendly smile. He wished fervently that he hadn't walked headfirst into a wall right in front of her. When he returned to their booth, Daisy had almost finished her next drink.

"I saw you bang your head," she laughed as he sat down.

"I was afraid you'd say that. At least the nice lady came to my rescue."

"You mean Lucy?"

"I don't know – do I?"

Daisy leaned forward conspiratorially. "Did you see her hand?"

Sigurdsson frowned. "The one she kept hidden? I thought maybe she had a broken wrist, or something."

"Try to have a look. I don't think she'd be angry with me for telling you. She performs in the freak show, after all."

"I read about that. Is it really still running?"

"Ooh, you *must* go and see it! I'll go and get you a flyer for it."

She darted across to the bar once again, returning seconds later with a photocopied sheet of A5 paper.

"It's on every fortnight. They've got a bearded lady, a merman, an alien foetus in a jar…" She handed him the flyer.

Doctor Mephisto's Notorious Showcase of the Curious

A collection of Abnormalities, Oddities
and other Strange Wonderments

Returning for your Viewing Pleasure at the
Salvation Leisure Centre
Every Second Friday, commencing at Ye Witching Hour

"I bet this is *exactly* your sort of thing," he muttered, turning the page over to see if there was any more information – there wasn't.

"Yep! I can't wait to see it. It's tomorrow night!"

"Who on earth is 'Doctor Mephisto'?"

"He's, well, he's the host – like a sort of PT Barnum character, I think. It's all a silly act, of course. I think in real life he's something to do with the museum. I've never met him, so I've no idea what to expect. It was the landlord here who told me about the show."

Sigurdsson put the advertisement back down on the table, confident he wouldn't be attending. "Anyway, Daisy, now that I have a chronic concussion, I should probably be getting back to–"

"Oh, are you coming to see our show?"

It was the waitress, Lucy. With one hand, she reached out to pick up the flyer. With the other she collected their empty rum and coke tumblers. This was an impressive feat, because her other hand wasn't a hand. Instead, her left arm simply tapered into a long, thin appendage, almost like a tentacle.

"I was just telling him about it, Lucy. He's definitely going to watch, aren't you, Chris?"

He tried not to stare at the unusual deformity. "Err, yes, I'll be there. Are you… involved with the show?"

She smiled. "You mean am I performing? Oh yes. I'll be showing off my party trick." She put down the flyer and transferred the glasses to her other hand so that she could wiggle the disfigured limb. "I'm pretty much the star attraction these days." A sadness entered her voice. "The island is falling to pieces around us, but people still come here to see the famous Octopus Girl."

Sigurdsson didn't respond. His mind was racing, trying to work out where he'd heard that name before.

POSSIBLE CULT MEMBERS

"Miss… er…" he began.

"It's Chen."

"Miss Chen, I'm a detective. I'm trying to find a missing person." He once again took out the photograph. "Do you remember this man, by any chance?"

The woman who called herself Octopus Girl bent down to peer at the snapshot.

"No, I'm sorry," she said after a pause. Her voice was accentless. "Is he in trouble?"

"Maybe," Sigurdsson replied, wondering how he could possibly bring up the subject of the cult. Perhaps the show *was* the cult, or at least somehow connected. "I didn't think they had these sorts of things nowadays," he said, gesturing at the flyer.

"What, 'freak shows'? Yes, it's quite rare to see one in this day and age. All the more reason to come and pay us a visit."

She winked at him and sauntered off.

Freak show. What an awful phrase. This woman was clearly far from freakish. He had a hundred questions for her. Like why on earth her pseudonym appeared on a note on David Lithgow's desk. But now was perhaps not the right time; he felt woozy, maybe from the booze, or maybe from the bang on the head.
It took him another three rounds of drinks before he could finally persuade Daisy to head back to her hotel, which turned out to be a B&B very similar to the Marine View. To his surprise, she tried to kiss him, but he politely declined, telling her he'd see her at the show the next day and wishing her the best of luck in the ghost train.

By the time he made it back to his own hotel room, his head was spinning. Only one day into his investigation, and Salvation had already dragged him deep, too deep, into its unique insanity.

Eleven (The island)

Sigurdsson awoke groggily the next morning, certain that his sleep had been plagued by nightmares, but unable to remember any of them. The mist at his window was thicker than the day before, as though it was gathering outside, straining at the glass.

It was 09:07 when he descended the stairs. He could smell and hear bacon frying as he sat down in the small serving area. "Sorry I'm a little late up," he called towards the kitchen. "I hope you aren't having to cook a special one just for me?"

Doug didn't respond until he brought the food out a few minutes later. "Don't worry, you're my only guest," the old man said, smiling wistfully as he deposited the steaming plate onto the plastic tablecloth. Sigurdsson was starving, but as he began to eat, flashes of his dark dreams returned, and the thought of the meat and gristle was suddenly abhorrent.

The women had been horribly mutilated, in some cases having body parts swapped between them and stitched crudely back into place

He picked at the beans and egg, glancing around at the quaint, chintzy décor as he tried to clear his mind. There were ornaments and vases on every available surface. The walls were covered in floral wallpaper, and here and there hanging plates depicted rural scenes, ducks in flight and, of course, rabbits. Like the pub he had visited the previous night, the place felt like a time capsule from the 1970s. He wondered about Doug, why he lived alone, whether he had had a wife, whether she had died. Whether he retained all of this bric-a-brac to try to preserve some fragment of her memory.

"Not too hungry then?" asked his host, interrupting his reverie.

Sigurdsson decided to keep his musings to himself. "It defeated me, I'm afraid. Doug, I might need to be in and out quite a bit over the coming days. It's probably better if you don't go to the trouble of making me breakfast unless I ask for it. Will that be okay?"

"Aye, lad, no problem. You can come and go as you please. The breakfast's no bother though – it gives me something to do." Once again, a sorrowful smile appeared beneath Doug's abundant moustache.

Sigurdsson made his apologies, suddenly desperate to leave that melancholy house.

It was only as he walked through the mist, the frigid air gnawing at him like something ravenous, that he remembered he was heading towards a house that was much, much worse.

As he approached Smalley Lane, he spotted a corner shop down a nearby side street and took a detour to pick up some supplies. A pre-packed sandwich, some crisps, a chocolate bar, a microwaveable meal; not exactly bursting with nutrition, but they would keep him going while he ploughed through as much of Lithgow's work as he could. Some kids ran past him as he left the store, their laughter sounding eerily out of place before it was swallowed by the mist. He realised that they were the first children he had seen since arriving back on the island.

Spitt's youngest victim, Alice Goldsmith, had been just fifteen when she was murdered and eviscerated

The worst thing about the house was how inconsequential it looked. A nondescript terrace, standing obliviously in the middle of the street, like the victim of a cruel trick that had defiled it forever without its knowledge or complicity.

But, as he stepped once again across the threshold, an aura of gleeful malice seemed to envelop him, and he was gripped by the insane notion that the house *did* understand, that in some way it had endorsed the atrocities committed by its former resident.

Later I became convinced he meant the house itself

And then it was gone, and he was standing alone in a living room that was wallpapered with a man's madness.

He began to read.

Twelve (The house)

Three hours later, only one piece had particularly resonated with him. It was a strangely detached passage, almost like an English student's literary analysis.

Heart of The Matter

For those that do not know the tragic story of The Minotaur, a brief synopsis.

As he battled his brothers for control of the island of Crete, Minos prayed to Poseidon to send him a snow-white bull as a sign of the god's support in his struggle. The creature appeared, and Minos duly emerged victorious; but after claiming the throne, Minos chose not to sacrifice the animal to appease his god, and Poseidon was enraged. The deity cursed Minos's wife, Pasiphae, to fall helplessly in love with the bull. Consumed by her unnatural cravings, she convinced the artisan Daedalus to construct an artificial cow in which she could hide, and thereby copulate with the beast. Daedalus obliged, and the device did its job perfectly.

Unfortunately, the encounter caused Pasiphae to fall pregnant.

When the child – named Asterion – was born with the head of a bull and the body of a man, Minos was so appalled that he banished the wretched infant to a huge labyrinth, designed by none other than Daedalus himself. Every seven years, as punishment for killing one of his sons during the war, Minos forced the vanquished Athenians to offer seven young men and seven young women as sacrifices to Asterion, who became known as the Minotaur. The helpless youths entered the fiendish maze… and never emerged.

After years of compliance with this monstrous tithe, Theseus, the son of the Athenian king Aegeus, could stand it no longer. He volunteered to enter the labyrinth himself and slay the feared monster. His father consented on the condition that Theseus would hoist a white sail upon his return home – this way, if he saw a black sail, Aegeus would know that his son had failed and been slaughtered by the beast.

Armed with the sword of Aegeus and a ball of thread woven by Ariadne, Theseus navigated the maze and slew the dreaded Minotaur; but upon his return home, he neglected to raise the white sail. When he arrived back in Athens, it was to the dreadful news that his distraught father had hurled himself to his death in the cruel waters of the ocean… giving the Aegean Sea its name.

The tale casts the Minotaur as a spider-like horror lurking at the centre of a great, dark web, occupying a structure designed to efficiently funnel its prey into his waiting jaws.

But is this not in fact the barbaric tale of the exile of an unwanted child? Asterion was condemned to a terrible existence, plodding the corridors of an impossible maze, hungry and alone in the gloom. Perhaps he had no choice but to feast upon the 'sacrifices' to sate his intolerable hunger. Perhaps he even tried to communicate with them, before they attacked him with revulsion and terror in their eyes. Cast out as an infant, unloved, reviled, treated as an undesirable freak, the Minotaur's fate was to live in exile until he was callously butchered by the belligerent Theseus.

It is hard to view the tragic end of Theseus's quest as anything but the cruellest sort of poetic justice. Indeed, perhaps his fate could be argued to be the worse of the two – in death, the Minotaur escaped the misery of its woeful life within the labyrinth, while Theseus was doomed to forever carry the burden of guilt for the death of his father.

But when one considers the maze not as the Minotaur's home, but instead as its prison, one perhaps wonders why its architect, Daedalus, is not viewed as the true villain of the story. I have searched in vain for an adaptation of the narrative where Daedalus himself is cast into the maze, starving slowly to death as he wanders within the bowels of his own devious construction… but so far, I have found nothing. The enduring myth has, strangely, allowed its primary antagonist to escape any punishment for his crimes.

Sigurdsson read it twice, different elements drawing his attention each time. The mention of freaks and abnormalities seemed to reference Dr Mephisto's show; perhaps he ought to go and see it later, after all? He sensed again that there was some connection he was missing between Lithgow's writing and the mysterious troupe.

And what about the idea of imprisonment? Spitt had willingly forced himself into a cell, then killed himself to escape its confines. The house, this house, a prison for those poor women, before death granted them merciful release… just like the Minotaur. But of course, this was a concept that could be extrapolated forever; the island as a prison for its inhabitants, who could only leave its shores in a ferryboat operated by a murderous lunatic; our mortal bodies as prisons for all of us, consigning us to age and frailty and bereavement and dementia…

Sigurdsson found himself in the kitchen once again, staring at Spitt's picture.

Life was a dark maze, full of wrong turns. Around some of them lurked monsters

An idea gripped Sigurdsson, and he turned to the pile of papers he had arranged on the table the previous day, leafing excitedly through the stack of maps. Representations of the island, but with unfamiliar road networks.

Or perhaps a different sort of system altogether.

He called Mason, who answered almost instantly.

"Hi, Chris."

"Do you have tunnels under the island? An old catacomb or something?"

"What, is that where you think we'll find Lithgow's body?"

"Maybe. I've been looking at the maps he drew… I think maybe they're depicting something underground, rather than on the surface."

"I'm sorry, Chris. We don't have any tunnels or caves or anything like that. Just a crappy little island with a LOT of water around it. I know you think I'm giving up too easily, but trust me, *that's* where Lithgow will be. Not in a secret cavern. He'll be in the water, probably in the bay, like Vic Valiant was."

"Yeah, and you *found* Valiant, remember?"

"Yes. And I really hope we find Lithgow too. Look, I do appreciate your help. I'm sorry I was off with you yesterday. I just…" A sigh took the place of whatever she had been about to say. "If I can get some spare time today I'll come and see you at the house. I don't like the thought of you cooped up in there on your own. The place is fucking creepy."

"I'll be fine. But yes, it would be great to get your help with this. And–" He had been about to say that it would be nice to see her again, but she interrupted.

"Chris, someone's just come into the station. I'm the bloody receptionist these days too, so I'd better go. Speak later."

He listened to her hang up. He thought about her, as he had done countless times over the past five years. Then he returned to scrutinising the maps.

If not underground tunnels, then what? Or did Lithgow simply like drawing mazes?

With Spitt lurking at the centre like a bloated, grinning spider

He made himself a cup of tea and picked at the sandwich while he moved on to other documents. Before long he had found another one that intrigued him, this one a transcript of an interview that ran across several pages. The content was a discussion about the Spitt murders, covering facts with which Sigurdsson was already familiar. But the heading at the top of the first page was what grabbed his attention.

Interview with Donald Armitage, 19 February 2014

Armitage had said he had never spoken to Lithgow.

Why would the old policeman lie?

He thought about the strange note, its list of four names: Donald Armitage, Octopus Girl, someone called Marion

Weisberg, and Edward Hardacre. It was time to give the island's owner another try.

The phone at Hardacre's house on the mainland rang and rang, like it had the previous day. But this time, the phone at his house on the island was answered on the third ring.

"Hello?" A woman's voice, sounding slightly surprised at the call.

"Hi. Is Edward Hardacre available please?"

"Yes. Um, I mean, what's this about?"

"I'd prefer to discuss it with him, if you don't mind."

"Oh." The woman sounded young, and now also somewhat put out. "Let me see."

There was no sound for about half a minute, and then a different voice addressed him, deep and gravelly. "Who is this?"

"My name is Chris Sigurdsson. Is this Edward Hardacre?"

"Yes." Hardacre's tone was clipped, with a faint Yorkshire accent.

"I'm a private detective, investigating a missing persons case, here on your island. It would be really helpful if I could speak with you."

Hardacre breathed out but did not reply.

"The missing man, David Lithgow, was writing a book about the island's history. Did he approach you?"

More breathing, before Hardacre finally responded. "Mr… Seegson, was it?" He continued before Sigurdsson could correct him. "I'm not sure how I can help you with this. I don't know any writers."

"I'm trying to speak with everyone that I think Mr Lithgow may have contacted." No need to tell him about the note bearing his name just yet. No need to tell him about the house.

"Okay. But you've got to appreciate that you've called me out of the blue, on my first day back on the island in weeks. If I'm going to talk to you, I'd prefer at least to see some ID, so I know you're a… legitimate operation."

"Would it be helpful if I came to see you in person?"

"It isn't really the best time for me," Hardacre answered after another long, breathy pause.

"Mr Hardacre, I know this is a strange call to receive out of nowhere, but David Lithgow's wife is distraught. That's why she's hired me. David suffers from bipolar disorder, and we're very worried about his safety. Even a few minutes of your time could be vital in locating him."

Hardacre's laboured breathing was the only response. In Sigurdsson's mind, he pictured an overweight man, or perhaps someone with a respiratory condition. Then his nightmares came back to him once again, and he saw instead a deformed creature, lying on a gurney, kept alive only by a wickedly complex breathing apparatus that protruded from its body like an obscene parasite. The thing's chest rose and fell as shallow breaths wracked its feeble body, like sobs. He shuddered and blinked the image away.

"Okay," Hardacre replied eventually. "If you've managed to find my number I'm sure you can get the address. I'll be here for the next few hours."

Sigurdsson was getting used to people hanging up on him.

Thirteen (Edward Hardacre's residence)

Hardacre had been right: finding the address was easy. It was in the northwest corner of the island, about a mile beyond the northern boundary of the theme park. As the main street curved towards the bay, a gravel path veered off to the left, and Sigurdsson proceeded along it at a sedate jog, not wanting to appear breathless and sweaty when he arrived. The road led through a scattering of trees, all of them stricken with the same greyish mould that afflicted the vegetation on the other side of the island. On a whim, he reached out to touch one of the blighted leaves, and it crumbled like the wing of a moth.

After a short while, the path crested a hill, and then led downwards towards Hardacre's home. Compared with the rest of the island, the house was grand, its impressive stature and surrounding lawns giving the impression of a country estate. But as he approached the squat, buff-coloured structure, Sigurdsson could see that the brickwork was crumbling, the roof tiles repaired here and there with cheap strips of flashing, the lawns unkempt and overgrown. He wondered about Hardacre, about how much of his family's fortune remained.

The front door had a brass knocker in the shape of a rabbit's head, requiring the visitor to grip its ears and bash the animal's skull against the sturdy white-painted wood. Sigurdsson rang the bell instead.

The door was opened by a pretty woman dressed in fluorescent pink running attire, her dark hair scraped back into a ponytail. "Oh," she said, looking him up and down as though disappointed. "Are you the detective?"

"That's right," Sigurdsson replied. "And you must be Mrs Hardacre?"

She looked uncomfortable and didn't reply to his question. Instead she leaned back into the house to call Hardacre's name, then hurried away without giving Sigurdsson another glance. He turned to watch her as she jogged past the large white Range Rover that was parked on the driveway, her feet crunching on the gravel. She disappeared over the same hill he had descended. Was she a girlfriend, perhaps? Or a family member?

Hardacre himself appeared moments later. He was a stout man, about Sigurdsson's height but with much wider shoulders and a thick frame, like a rugby player gone to fat. His tanned face had a meaty sturdiness to it, resembling a chunk of wood, dense and lined and imposing. A cigar hung from his mouth, and behind the plumes of smoke that curled from its tip, his expression was unreadable. He was wearing a nondescript assortment of expensive-looking brown clothes, dressed exactly like a businessman on his day off.

"You're the detective?" he asked, echoing the woman's question.

Sigurdsson nodded, and produced his identification. Hardacre took it from him and studied it for a while before handing it back. "Okay," he said, nodding as he seemed to reach a decision. "Let's head to the veranda."

He led Sigurdsson around the outside of the house, as if he didn't like the idea of inviting the detective inside. Maybe he was worried about allowing an investigator to study his choices of décor, his furniture, to formulate opinions about him based upon his possessions. Maybe he was a control freak. Or maybe he was having a sneaky weekend break with his mistress and didn't want Sigurdsson to see the evidence.

At the rear of the house was a pleasant patio area where several sets of metal tables and chairs were arranged beneath a striped awning. Hardacre gestured for Sigurdsson to sit at one of them, and then disappeared into the house before returning with two glasses and a bottle of whisky.

"None for me, thanks," said Sigurdsson.

Hardacre looked genuinely surprised. "Are you sure? That's a twenty-five-year-old Glenfarclas, you know."

"Maybe another time," the detective replied, trying to smile graciously. In his mind, he added *when it's a little later than two in the afternoon.*

"Suit yourself," replied Hardacre, pouring a large dram without offering Sigurdsson anything else to drink. He crushed out his cigar in an ashtray as he continued. "I don't spend a lot of time on the island these days, but I like to have some of this in stock for whenever I do visit." His breathing was loud and laboured, as it had been on the phone, and Sigurdsson looked with distaste at the remnants of the cigar.

"And is this a business trip or just a summer holiday?"

"Oh, very much a holiday. My accountant doesn't trust me to handle my business affairs." Hardacre smiled, but Sigurdsson thought he caught something in the expression; maybe a twist of bitterness, or even a haunted aspect, as though Hardacre's 'business affairs' were keeping him awake at night.

Sigurdsson probed gently. "How long have you owned the island?"

Hardacre stared at the whisky in his hand, avoiding eye contact. "I inherited it when my father died. That was over twenty years ago."

"Do you collect rent from all the people who live here?"

"Very few of them; we had to sell most of the houses soon after I took over. My main income is from the gift shops and the ferry fares these days... not that either represents a particularly big revenue stream anymore."

Hardacre swirled the dark liquid in his glass.

"It must be difficult for you," Sigurdsson said. "I suppose the island was much more popular back when your father bought it?"

"Of course, it was," Hardacre retorted with sudden vehemence. "And now... well, you've seen the place. Who would want to come here when they could spend their summer on a beach in

Portugal?" As he said the word 'here', he raised his hands as if to indicate the whole of the island, not the first time Sigurdsson had seen that despairing gesture from one of Salvation's inhabitants.

"I suppose you must get some history buffs visiting the museum?"

"Yes, the museum doesn't do too badly, I suppose. People still seem to be interested in the bombing and wandering through the ruins." He fell silent again, perhaps ruminating on the village, its buildings long ago reduced to the blackened husks that Sigurdsson had seen in photographs.

"I haven't been to the village," Sigurdsson said. "Why would the Germans attack somewhere like this, do you think?"

Hardacre smiled grimly. "You must have heard the rumours about the rabbits? The story goes that the island was a secret poison gas development site; the convalescent home was a smokescreen for its real purpose. The Nazis found out, somehow, and bombed the place to smithereens… but some of the test subjects survived, and bred, and now the place is overrun with their descendants." He scoffed. "It's all nonsense of course, about the gas, but I think that mystery was part of what attracted my father to it. He fell in love with Salvation's history, its potential… even with those bloody rabbits."

Sigurdsson realised that he hadn't seen a single rabbit near Hardacre's house. "Don't you like them yourself?"

Hardacre snorted a laugh but didn't reply. Instead he rose suddenly from his seat, leaving the whisky glass behind as he headed back inside the house without a word.

What a strange man, thought Sigurdsson. A long while passed, and he wondered whether Hardacre was even going to reappear.

Then the patio doors opened, and a monster emerged instead.

Sigurdsson leapt from his seat, stumbling backwards and nearly falling to the ground as the hellish creature bounded towards him in a blur of hair, muscle and teeth. A scream bubbled up from deep inside him, born in a place of animal terror that he had managed to suppress for many years. His hands fumbled at the pocket where he kept the bulky torch that could also double as a weapon.

Then the beast jumped up and licked his face. Sigurdsson choked down a scream, and felt his horror subside.

It was, of course, a dog. A monstrous dog, that stood taller than him on its hind legs. Its slate-coloured fur was matted and scruffy, giving it a mongrel appearance, but beneath this shabby coat was a lean, powerful physique, like an athlete in peak condition. Or a perfect killing machine.

Hardacre appeared in the doorway, chuckling as he sauntered towards them. The dog was dancing a figure of eight at Sigurdsson's feet, repeatedly jumping up to paw at him as the detective tried to keep it at bay. Its eyes gleamed with manic excitement.

"Sit!" Hardacre barked abruptly, and the immense hound turned briefly towards its master as though contemplating disobedience. Then it sank reluctantly to the ground, staring up at Sigurdsson with saliva glistening around its lips. It looked like something spawned in an irradiated city, a feral scavenger that would be more at home stalking the blasted streets of a post-apocalyptic wasteland, hunting for meat.

"He's a beauty, isn't he?" Hardacre beamed as he bent to pat the animal's head. "An Irish wolfhound, if you didn't know. You don't seem like much of a 'dog person', detective."

Sigurdsson tried to recover his composure. "His size is… a little intimidating."

Hardacre laughed again, a cruel edge to the sound. "Yes, I suppose that's why I bought him. They're the world's tallest dog breed, you know. But Anax here is particularly big, even for his kind."

"Anax?"

"One of the giants in Greek mythology. It means 'king' or 'leader'."

"He's definitely… a specimen. But I thought you didn't allow dogs on the island?"

Hardacre took another sip from his glass and smiled unpleasantly. "If you can't break your own rules, what's the point of being in charge, eh? And besides, Anax loves it here. I take him hunting in the woods. You asked if I like the rabbits? The answer is no. I can't stand the vermin. But Anax likes them, don't you, boy?"

Hardacre once again ruffled the dog's head, and the creature seemed to mirror his owner's grin, perhaps gleefully anticipating the next hunt. Sigurdsson imagined his teeth crunching through fur and bone, and shuddered.

"So, you were saying something about a missing person?" Hardacre said, seeming pleased that he had managed to unsettle his visitor.

Sigurdsson sat back down and extracted the photograph from his wallet. He slid it across the table to Hardacre. "This man, David Lithgow, has been living on the island. He was renting Leonard Spitt's house from you."

Hardacre's expression darkened at the mention of the name. "Oh. Now I remember. I've spoken to DI Mason about this already."

"Yes. She mentioned that you'd like to have the house cleared out soon, so that you can find a new tenant."

"That's right. I can't afford to leave the house empty indefinitely." Hardacre met Sigurdsson's gaze, seeming to bristle at the direction of the detective's questions. The dog watched intently, his dangling tongue dripping saliva onto the floor.

"Mr Lithgow was writing a book, about Spitt. That's why he wanted to rent that particular house."

"I see. I didn't realise. I try not to advertise the fact that a serial killer lived there, as I'm sure you can understand."

"You mean you don't tell people that they're renting a murder house?" Sigurdsson replied, aghast.

Hardacre's expression remained taciturn. "I'm not sure what that has to do with your missing person, detective," he said evenly.

Sigurdsson bit down his irritation and held Hardacre's stare. "So, when Lithgow first rented the house, did you have any interaction with him?"

Hardacre shook his head dismissively. "No, it's all handled through a letting agent. I don't even know who's living in my properties. The first I heard of Lithgow was when DI Mason called me to discuss his disappearance."

"Have you seen the house? How he left it?"

"No. I don't like to go there. The place gives me the creeps."

"But Mason told you about the writing he left everywhere."

"Yes, she said a lot of his belongings had been left behind."

"You were mentioned in his notes."

Hardacre's eyebrows lifted slightly, but he said nothing. Sigurdsson could feel the dog's eyes fixed on him, as if he was trying to figure out whether he would soon be permitted to eat him.

"Your name was on a list titled 'possible cult members'. I wondered if that meant anything to you?"

Hardacre snorted again and shook his head. "A cult? What, like the Manson Family? I'm sorry, Mr Seegson, but it doesn't sound like this man, Lithgow, was of particularly sound mind."

"It's Sigurdsson. So you've never heard of a cult operating on the island?"

"Nothing of the sort. Are you sure he wasn't working on a piece of fiction?"

Sigurdsson reached over to take back the photograph. "What about Spitt?" he asked as he did so. "I assume you met him? You said you receive the income from the ferries."

Hardacre shifted uncomfortably in his seat. "He worked for my father. Did odd jobs for us, around this house sometimes. So yes, I met him a few times."

"What did you think, when you found out about the killings? I suppose it was quite a scandal."

Hardacre shrugged. "It was… unfortunate. We were already struggling with the costs of this place. Now we had another reason for people not to come here. Although actually the media frenzy did us a bit of good, in terms of publicity. People are strange."

He finished off the contents of his glass, and immediately poured another.

"David Lithgow was certainly fascinated by the case," said Sigurdsson. "It seems odd that he wouldn't try to contact you, given the project he was working on."

Hardacre shrugged again, lighting up another cigar. "I'll say it again: people are strange, detective. Now, is there anything else I can help you with, or—"

He stopped in mid-sentence as Anax suddenly rose to his feet, growling. The giant hound was staring off into the distance, and Hardacre followed his eye line.

"What's that, boy? Spotted a rabbit, have you?" Hardacre gripped the beast's collar, although the dog showed no sign of struggling to run away. He simply fixed its gaze on a point somewhere behind Sigurdsson and bared his vicious incisors.

Sigurdsson turned, but could see nothing amongst the expanse of long grass behind them. Anax continued to growl, the sound guttural and frightening.

Then he heard Hardacre hiss something quietly into his pet's ear. It was the word 'kill'.

The dog bolted into the undergrowth with terrifying speed. Sigurdsson watched, transfixed, as he charged towards a spot about a hundred metres away, bending to bite at something in the grass, twisting, doubling back, attacking the same point once again.

Seconds later, the blur of violence was over, and Anax was trotting back smugly towards them with the mangled corpse of a rabbit clamped between his jaws. He deposited the shredded carcass at the bottom of the patio, and then sat next to it, wagging his tail happily. A crimson trail marked the route he had taken back across the lawn.

"Good boy!" enthused Hardacre, rising from his seat to pet and play with the dog, which was now rolling on the ground and pawing at his master, blood still flecking his lips. Sigurdsson watched the perverse display, feeling slightly ill.

"Mr Hardacre, I'll leave you in peace for now," he said, rising to his feet. "Here's my card. If you think of anything that might be relevant, then please don't hesitate to contact me."

"Yes, fine, just leave it on the table," Hardacre replied, still wrestling with his oversized pet. The dog looked quite capable of biting his owner's head off if he wanted to, but they both seemed happy enough; certainly, happier than the mauled rabbit that was leaking gore onto the flagstones.

Sigurdsson headed back up the gravel driveway, reflecting on another odd encounter. Hardacre had seemed more like an eccentric, retired military commander than a shrewd businessman. There was definitely something going on, under the surface; financial troubles perhaps, and maybe an extramarital affair. And his colossal dog was certainly far from normal. But did any of those amount to anything more than irrelevant idiosyncrasies? Hardacre's only tangible connection to the case was Lithgow's note, linking him to some sort of cult; a subject that once again had been stonewalled. Was it really nothing more than the fabrication of a troubled mind?

Sigurdsson had learned to rely on his instincts, over the years. And he could feel, strongly, that something was being withheld from him. He thought about the walls of the house, covered in words, clues, leads, possibilities. The problem was not that he didn't have a thread to grasp at; the problem was that he had far, far too many.

The only answer was to be patient, to continue to sift through the vast amount of data that Lithgow had left behind. To stay focused. Concentrate.

But as he walked, his thoughts kept drifting back to Hardacre's grotesque pet. He glanced back over his shoulder, half expecting to see him bounding after him up the hill.

Kill

As Hardacre's house disappeared over the horizon, Sigurdsson couldn't help quickening his pace.

Fourteen (The house)

Sigurdsson thought he might encounter Hardacre's visitor returning in the opposite direction, but he didn't. In fact, he didn't see another soul all the way back to the house, as though the island's inhabitants had simply dissolved into the mist.

He unlocked the door and stepped inside, faced immediately with two more doors: one leading into a room quite literally wallpapered in mysteries, and the other opening only to the empty, oppressive horror of the basement. Strange how he thought of the house as Lithgow's, but the basement very much as Leonard Spitt's.

As Sigurdsson turned towards the living room door, he saw a note stuck to its outside. For a crazy moment he thought Lithgow had returned, and simply carried on where he left off, capturing his thoughts on paper and pinning them to any available surface. Then he read the note, and realised it was from Mason.

'Came but you weren't here. Fridge looked depressing, so I've left you some food. Good luck. C. x'

His eyes lingered on the 'x', knowing that he was reading far too much into the hastily scrawled symbol, that it was probably inscribed out of habit without even a conscious thought. He knew his feelings were pathetically teenage, but he allowed the thought of her to fill him with a pleasant glow; the idea that she had been here seemed to temporarily neutralise the cold malevolence of the house.

He walked straight through to the kitchen and found her gift on the worktop, smelling the fish and chips before he even unwrapped the paper. He tore open the greasy parcel and ate, suddenly ravenous. He thought of Anax, of hot blood and rabbit flesh sliding down the dog's throat, but even that didn't deter him from gulping down the rest of the food.

He opened the bin to get rid of the paper and the little plastic fork and stopped. The remnants of a second portion of fish and chips had already been thrown away; Mason must have arrived with a meal for two and ended up eating hers alone. He felt a pang of regret, and almost without thinking, he took out his phone and dialled her number. She didn't answer. He listened to her recorded message, then ended the call before the beep. Then he rang again. Maybe he just wanted to hear her voice for a second time. This time he waited for the tone and said, 'thanks for the food', then hung up.

He stood, staring out of the window, into the empty yard. He felt suddenly very alone. He thought about calling Mason again. He thought about calling Priya.

Instead he went into the living room and continued to read.

Definitions:

Nexus
1. A connection or series of connections linking two or more things
2. A central or focal point

Convergence
1. The process or state of converging

Converge
1. (of lines) To tend to meet at a point
2. (of a series) Approximate in the sum of its terms towards a definite limit

Vehicle
1. A thing used for transporting people or goods, especially on land, such as a car, lorry, or cart
2. A thing used to express, embody, or fulfil something

World

1. The earth, together with all of its countries and peoples
2. 2. Human and social interaction
3. 3. Another planet like the earth

Vessel

1. A ship or large boat
2. A hollow container, especially one used to hold liquid, such as a bowl or cask

Spitt's victims:

Fiona Prudence
- Born in Essex but moved to Barnstaple when she was 22 to live with her future husband
- Worked as a travel agent in the town centre
- Her husband was investigated after he reported that she had not returned home from a night out with friends in 1989, but no charges were brought against him, and the case was never solved
- At 42 when she was abducted, she was Spitt's oldest victim
- Blonde hair
- Slim build

Ella Wright
- Born and raised in Woolacombe, where she was employed part time as a care worker
- Had three children, raising them singlehandedly after the death of her husband in a construction accident; they were aged 11, 9 and 6 when she disappeared
- Was known to enjoy walking her Jack Russell on the beach
- Neither she nor the dog were found after they went missing in 1990
- Blonde hair
- Slim build

Gabby Kowalcyzk
- Lived with her parents in Ilfracombe, having recently started working as a policewoman
- Known as a lively character who enjoyed the local nightlife, and was last seen by friends catching a taxi home in 1991 – the cab driver was later questioned and eliminated from the enquiry
- Had recently begun dyeing her hair platinum blonde
- Slim build

Kate Byrne
- Worked as a GP in Minehead, having relocated from Bristol to accept the position
- A divorcee who lived alone, her marriage breaking down shortly after the death of the couple's first and only child during childbirth
- Enjoyed hiking and long walks, and disappeared in 1993 during one such outing
- Blonde hair
- Slim build

Carol Schofield
- Employed as a secondary school teacher in Barnstaple, where she was born
- Reportedly suffered from anxiety, anorexia, and stress, and had been off work for several months prior to her disappearance in 1994
- Left behind two children and a husband, who mounted an extensive media campaign and promised a reward for any information about her whereabouts
- Blonde hair
- Very slight build

Alice Goldsmith
- Born in Westward Ho! and still living there at the time of her disappearance

- Fifteen when she went missing in 1995, during her final year at Great Oaks High School
- A local man was arrested in connection with her murder, but charges were never brought against him, and her case remained unsolved until Spitt's confession
- Blonde hair
- Slim build
- Believed to have been Spitt's final victim before his death in 1996

He devoured page after page, filling his mind with more and more details of the Spitt case. The process was not pleasant, as if he was deliberately allowing a disease into his brain. He could only imagine what months of immersion in this toxic narrative had done to Lithgow's psyche.

Behind the words, sometimes typewritten, sometimes scrawled in Lithgow's frenzied style, the missing man's voice was glaringly inconsistent. Sometimes he wrote with cold precision, like a surgeon wielding a scalpel. In other passages he wrote with warmth and humanity, as in a peculiar, handwritten account of the death of a pet that he and Erina had owned.

When we got back from our holiday the rabbit had stopped eating.

We'd had Bobby the house rabbit for just over three years, having bought him when we lived in the flat. The plan had been for him to live outside when we moved to somewhere with a garden, but we hadn't had the heart to exile him, so instead he lived in a hutch in the spare bedroom. We let him out during the day, and he had the full run of the room, as well as the landing, and usually our room too. The place tended to look like a bit of a zoo as a result. He was fully litter-trained of course, but that didn't stop him from leaving a few droppings here and there, and treading his hay all over the place, and nibbling at everything. Most of the old clothes I own have his bite marks in them.

Every so often we'd let him out into the garden, and he used to go crazy. Rabbits do this thing called a 'binky' when they're really excited, where they spring up into the air and throw their back end and head in different directions. The first time you see it they look like they've gone completely mad, but once you understand its meaning it's a lovely sight – a bit like your baby smiling, I suppose. He used to sprint up and down the garden in sudden bursts, 'binkying' all over the grass, looking like he might explode with glee.

(We never really talked about children. There was this... understanding, I suppose, that now was somehow not the time. Sometimes I used to try to start the conversation casually, as an interesting subject, but Erina always became withdrawn, monosyllabic, and I gradually got used to the fact that it wasn't something we ever spoke about.)

The first year we got him we didn't go away on holiday – we didn't want to leave him alone, so tiny and fluffy and dependent. But after we'd had one of our Sensible Chats and decided we had to get away from the house sometimes, otherwise we'd start to resent him, and we'd been away for a couple of long weekends and our neighbours had done a great job of looking after him, we thought we'd be okay to go on a longer trip. We'd saved and planned and discussed and debated, and ultimately, we had a lovely time in Greece.

When we got back, Roy and Denise said that he'd been fine, and we were relieved. But over the coming days, we noticed that his food bowl didn't seem to be going down very much. We switched to new pellets, but to no avail. He wasn't using his litter tray much either or drinking enough water. He was spending more and more time just lying in the hutch, not out exploring the house like he normally would, searching for expensive things to chew on.

We'd done lots of research when we got him, and we knew that rabbits are delicate little machines – a few days without food and their whole complex digestive system, more similar to that of a horse than that of a rodent, goes into irreversible shutdown.

His droppings became sad and compact and grey, and the vet gave us liquid food to syringe straight into his mouth. Normally any veterinary treatments, indeed any reason to pick him up, were met with frantic protests, Bobby scurrying away from us across the floor *until he was truly cornered. But this was much worse; now he simply sat there, forlorn and acquiescent in the hutch, and allowed us to manhandle him. He chewed and swallowed the food we squirted into his mouth and we raised our hopes that it would jump-start him, but it didn't. He wouldn't even eat his favourite little yoghurt drops, the ones we used to hide under empty toilet rolls for him to knock over and discover. The cardboard tubes remained untouched each night, and in the morning, we were greeted by the same sad cylindrical village in the hallway.*

He was dead ten days after we arrived back home, lying on his side in the hutch, eyes open and wide as if the end had still somehow surprised him. I'd have struggled to know what to do if I'd have found him, whether to bury him alone to spare you the heartbreak, or whether to wake you and explain gently that he had passed away, and that it was a good thing really because his suffering was over, and that he'd been a lovely pet and we'd always remember him, and then hug you while you cried and I tried not to.

As it was, you found him, and then I found you. You were huddled in the corner of the room, knees pressed into your chest, not even looking at him. I don't know which creature looked more tragic. You looked like you were trying to disappear into your dressing gown.

I sat with you for a while, holding you. When I picked him up, his stiffness was unexpected and unpleasant, and I didn't really know what I intended to do with him. In the end I put him in a shoebox and dug him a grave in the garden. I'd had family pets before, but my parents had always buried them, and I remember wondering as I slowly scooped out the earth with a trowel whether they'd buried Monty and Pepper (the cats) as deep, or in a shoe box, or maybe wrapped in a blanket. I thought about all the people and animals that had ever been buried, and how there must be many more skeletons than there are living people, and how if you could somehow invert the earth it would be terribly overcrowded. I wondered if the skeletons would fight brutally for space and territory like we do, or whether the deceased would make a more peaceful, accepting race. I thought about how our whole world stood upon the bones of our dead, and it seemed somehow repulsive.

I made a little headstone thing out of some pieces of Bobby's chew toys, but you said you didn't want to be sad every time you looked out at your garden, so I pulled it out and threw it away.

A year later, I read about Salvation, and all the rabbits running wild, and it seemed like the perfect place for us to go on holiday.

Sigurdsson felt uncomfortable as he read the very personal account. It was a relief when his phone rang, interrupting the sad tale, and when he saw that it was Mason, his heart swelled, just slightly.

"Thanks for the food," he said as he answered.

"You said that already," she replied. "I got your message. Where were you?"

"I went out to meet Edward Hardacre. He's an interesting man."

"Yeah, I've had the pleasure. Did you meet that fucking werewolf he keeps at the house?"

"You mean Anax? I wish you'd warned me about it. I thought it was going to eat me."

"There's something weird about a man who keeps a pet like that."

"There's something weird about pretty much everyone I meet on this island."

"You must like it, or you wouldn't keep coming back."

"Evidently there's something weird about me, too."

She laughed. "So… are you getting anywhere? Today has been quiet for a change, so I was thinking of coming to join you. Mitchell can look after the shop for me."

Sigurdsson remembered her deputy: sullen and taciturn, but dependable. "Actually, I was going to go to see a show tonight. Have you ever heard of Doctor Mephisto?"

"Oh, God. Is Bill still doing that drivel?"

"Bill?"

"'Doctor Mephisto' is the curator at the museum. His real name is William Cronin. He's a nice chap, bit of an oddball, knows everything there is to know about the island. He does the freak show thing in his spare time."

"I met the 'Octopus Girl' in a pub last night. That's how I heard about it. Do you know her?"

"I do. And do all the leads you're pursuing involve you meeting pretty waitresses in bars?"

She said it jokingly, but there was perhaps a slight twinge of jealousy in her voice. Perhaps.

"It's a long story. But Lithgow believes she was a member of a cult – I was hoping to ask her about it. Do you… want to join me?"

"Hang on. What cult?"

"Lithgow wrote something about a cult and listed its possible members. It might be nothing, but I want to check it out. That's why I went to visit Hardacre – his name appeared on the list too." Sigurdsson decided not to mention Armitage yet, because he knew Mason had a lot of respect for her predecessor.

"I've heard about the cult before, Chris. It's all nonsense, like I keep telling you. Just another crazy conspiracy theory someone has cooked up about this mad place."

"What do you know about it?"

She sighed. "Not much. I think it was tied to Saint Drogo's supposed healing powers… like they believed there was an *actual* spirit trapped inside the statue, and they were worshipping it, or something. I don't think it's going to help you to find Lithgow."

"It wasn't only the cult. He wrote about labyrinths, Carin. Drew maps and diagrams. I think he was searching for something. Maybe he found it?"

"This isn't fucking Indiana Jones, Chris."

"I'm going to the show anyway. If only so I can see the pretty waitress."

"In that case I'd better come along, to keep an eye on you. Where is it?"

"At the leisure centre, but it doesn't start until midnight."

"Bloody hell. That's way past my bedtime."

"Do you want to crack this case or not?"

"You're the only one who thinks there's a case to crack, I'm afraid."

"Meet you at the Cloak and Dagger at ten?"

"I'll be there. This sounds like the weirdest date ever."

"People keep saying that to me."

"That should probably tell you something."

He laughed and said goodbye and made sure he was the first to hang up for a change.

Sigurdsson glanced at his watch: 19:42. That gave him about an hour to carry on reading. He tore his mind away from thoughts of Mason (*date… she had said it was a date…*) and instead focused on studying the many pages of maps and the notes scrawled on them, all of which seemed to support his theory that Lithgow had been searching for the entrance to an underground cave network of some sort. He had marked dozens of places on the island, even drawing up diagrams purporting to capture the busiest areas in terms of rabbit activity, as though that might lead him to the most likely location.

Sigurdsson thought about the rabbits, burrowing beneath him, turning the rock of the island into a honeycomb. Thousands of openings, maybe more. Miles and miles of tiny tunnels… perhaps some of them intersected by a larger, manmade warren. Was that where Erina Brennan's estranged husband had gone? Had he followed his obsession deep into the earth?

A horrible thought gripped Sigurdsson then, of David Lithgow still alive, weeks after going missing. Lost underground. Starving, thirsty, and alone, in the darkness. Sigurdsson felt that same nauseous feeling once again, bubbling up within his throat, and immediately he could feel Spitt's eyes on him, even though the photograph was on the other side of the kitchen door.

He took a few deep breaths, remembering the debilitating effect of his anxiety attacks, and calmed himself. They weren't going to come back. That was in his past. The old, frightened Chris Sigurdsson was dead. He had been killed on this very island.

He glanced again at his watch. Shit. It was past nine o' clock, and he was still wearing his sweaty running clothes; he had to get back to the Marine View to change before heading out. Even if he left now, it would be a struggle to make it on time.

The show would be a useful break and would give him a chance to ask some important questions. But he felt certain that the answer was *here*: somewhere on these walls, amongst these pages. He felt a compelling urge to call Mason and cancel, to skip Mephisto's show, to stay here all night instead. Reading.

But the house would still be there the next day. A man's descent into insanity, freeze-framed.

He locked the door behind him and hurried out into the chill of the night.

Fifteen (The island)

Despite the rush, Sigurdsson arrived at the Cloak and Dagger slightly early, feeling clean and refreshed after a shower. Once again Mason was even earlier, waiting for him at the bar. She somehow managed to look stunning, and simultaneously like she hadn't made any effort at all. She was wearing jeans and a shirt, and had styled her hair slightly differently again, this time pushed back behind her ears, which had small plain studs in them. He liked her new haircut, he decided. Very much.

She waved him over. "I got you a J2O," she said, sliding him the bottle and a glass. "I thought we should stay dry while we're working a case tonight."

"I thought you said there was no case?" he retorted, pulling up a barstool.

"You know what I mean."

"Anyway, before we get to that, I haven't even had a chance to ask how you're doing. How's Holly?"

Mason's eyes lit up at the mention of her daughter. "Holly's great. She's nearly old enough to leave primary school, would you believe? She likes art. And *Frozen*."

"Tell her I said hello. Do you think she remembers me?"

"I'm sure she does," Mason said. Her eyes were the colour of chocolate.

"Err… and what about your mum?" Sigurdsson asked, suddenly aware of the silence.

Mason's expression stiffened. "Mum died," she said, bluntly.

"Oh God, I'm so sorry. What happened?"

"Cancer. Very fast. She didn't suffer for long. But it was hard on Holly and me. Especially after…" She trailed off, and he didn't press her to finish the sentence. They sat in silence for a few moments.

"She was a lovely woman," he said eventually.

"Thanks. Anyway, that was three years ago. How long has it been since we spoke, Chris? Four?"

"Five," he answered, too quickly.

"So how come you didn't call? I thought maybe we would keep in touch. But I suppose you're… busy with the agency?"

"Yes. We've got an office in London now."

He took out one of his business cards and handed it to her. She studied it and smiled.

"I'm impressed. I imagine it keeps you tied up, then?"

"It does. Although I have an assistant. Well, more of a partner, really. She's very good. Err, a work partner, I mean; she's not a… she's just my colleague." He realised he was babbling, and took a sip from his glass, willing the burning in his cheeks to subside.

"You mean you haven't met someone?"

She said it lightly, conversationally, but he could feel her eyes fixed on him. He shook his head.

"Nope. Other than Casper."

"Casper?"

"He's my Betta half." He laughed at his own joke. She just stared at him. "He's a Japanese fighting fish. They're called Bettas. That was a really good pun, I think you'll find."

"I'm sure," she said, deadpan. Then she laughed, and he felt strangely light-headed, and concentrated hard on drinking his J2O.

They talked for a while longer, reminiscing about the craziness of their previous case. They joked about Mitchell's grumpiness, and Mason told him about the 'jittery' new pathologist that had replaced the retired Hamish Leithauser. Sigurdsson told her a little about some of his recent cases, making sure to exaggerate any heroism or ingenuity he had displayed. She didn't fall for a word of it.

After a while, he pointed out that it was time to head to the show. She laughed again.

"Why do you wear a digital watch, Chris? Only children and hipsters wear those, you know."

"I… like to know the exact time."

"You always were very organised."

"Is that a nice way to say, 'you're a weirdo'?"

"Welcome to Salvation," she said, winking as they stood up and put on their jackets. There was hardly anyone left in the bar. Lucy, the 'Octopus Girl', wasn't working that night, of course; she was presumably getting ready for the show.

It took them only a few minutes to walk along the promenade to the leisure centre, which was a large grey cuboid behind the main Visitors' Centre. A huge pink rabbit beamed down at them from the side of the building, but what was supposed to be a welcoming smile looked more like a demented grin, its painted eyes following them eerily as they approached the entrance. Outside, a stooped figure waited, dressed in tattered rags that covered its body and face, like a leper. A sign next to this peculiar gatekeeper read 'Dr Mephisto's Showcase of the Curious: Entry Fee £10'. The hunched figure held out a hand as they approached, and Sigurdsson proffered a twenty-pound note, feeling decidedly uncomfortable when the creature bowed and grovelled, emitting a sinister cackle as it did so.

Mason looked amused as they headed inside.

All the lights were switched off in the spacious reception area, the only illumination coming from streetlights outside. A curtain had been hung over the main hallway, with 'WAIT HERE FOR YOUR OWN SAFETIE' painted onto it in large red letters. A few dozen people were already gathered, chatting and giggling.

"I won't lie… this is pretty cool," hissed Sigurdsson as they took up a place close to the reception desk. After a few minutes, the curtain suddenly parted, and a black man in a battered top hat emerged from behind it.

"That's Bill," whispered Mason.

"You mean Doctor Mephisto," Sigurdsson retorted, as the lights suddenly came on, and their host began to speak.

"Ladies and gentlemen," he intoned, grinning widely. He was wearing a threadbare black suit and carrying a cane, which he twirled theatrically as he spoke. Sigurdsson thought that he looked a little like Doctor Facilier from the Disney movie *The Princess and the Frog*. He didn't mention this to Mason, because she wouldn't have heard him; Mephisto's voice was booming through a small radio mic attached to his lapel, his deep mock-American growl pitched somewhere between Tom Waits and Darth Vader.

"Welcome to tonight's festivities," he continued, his tongue rolling around the letters like a snake behind his teeth. "If you enjoy being thrilled, excited, repulsed, exhilarated… you've come to the right place!" He did a little pirouette on the spot, and then slammed his cane into the ground, making several members of the audience jump.

"But first! A warning. Tonight, you will see things. Things that will make your head… spin." His purple bow tie rotated, seemingly of its own accord, and some of the audience laughed.

"It is *strongly* advised that anyone of a nervous disposition does not set foot beyond this curtain." He pointed his cane towards the cloth, which jerked and writhed as if something was hidden behind it, thrashing violently.

"Indeed, as you enter, my associate will present you with a special waiver, which you must sign before proceeding any further. It is a small legal formality, basically absolving me of any responsibility for ill effects, side effects, physical effects, mental effects, special effects, or any other ailments which you good people may suffer following exposure to the *horrors* that await you." He grinned even more widely at this point, his curled moustache seeming to twitch like something alive.

"But enough of the pleasantries… I'm sure you didn't come here to listen to little old me." He removed his top hat and clasped it solemnly in both hands, exposing a gleamingly bald head beneath. His gaze dropped, as though he was about to disclose something personal and poignant. "It's…" he murmured, and then paused for many seconds.

Then he cried "SHOWTIME!" and tossed his top hat into the air, and they were plunged into darkness once again. The curtain fell away behind him, revealing a corridor faintly lit by a series of patio lights. Mephisto caught his top hat as it fell, and scurried gleefully down the corridor beyond, turning right and darting through a pair of double doors. Mason and Sigurdsson followed him, along with the rest of the crowd, who were murmuring and chuckling amongst themselves.

Next to the doors, a sign read 'Follow the Doctor', and the same cringing servant awaited them, this time holding a stack of printed sheets. As they approached, Mephisto's assistant wordlessly handed them a form and a pen, jabbing at the paper to indicate where they should sign. Sigurdsson looked at the document. The only words on it were 'I CONSENT TO BEING TERRIFIED.' He smiled, signed it 'Mickey Mouse', and handed back the paper.

The doors led into the sports hall itself, which was again dimly lit, and had been cleverly partitioned by hanging curtains into a series of narrow 'passageways'. The bright red fabric reminded Sigurdsson of the Black Lodge in *Twin Peaks*. He hung back before entering, trying to spot Daisy in the crowd. She didn't seem to be there, but he did notice Hardacre, accompanied by the woman Sigurdsson had met at the house. Mercifully, Anax wasn't with them. They either didn't spot him or chose to ignore him as they passed by.

Inside the sports hall, Mephisto was waiting for them, leaning on his cane.

"Welcome all, and allow me to commend you on your bravery," he began, still smiling mischievously. "Before I introduce our first exhibit, I wanted to explain a little about the history of the travelling 'freak show'… although I do not particularly approve of the term. I prefer to think of what we do here as *a celebration of exceptional humans*."

He paced back and forth in front of them, every now and then stopping to address his monologue to a particular member of the crowd, or gesture extravagantly with the walking stick. He was an excellent showman.

"When they were first conceived in the sixteenth century, freak shows quickly became wildly popular. Even Charles I, the king of England, had one such exhibition in his court, famously featuring the conjoined twins, Lazarus and Joannes Baptista Colloredo. By the nineteenth century they had reached the peak of their popularity, and such travelling exhibits were a mainstay of western culture; particularly in America, where they were commonplace at circuses, amusement parks, and vaudeville. Now, we all know that Salvation's own amusement park may have seen better days... but I am proud and honoured to say that Doctor Mephisto's Showcase of the Curious is still going strong!"

Some of the audience clapped at this, and Mephisto bowed elegantly before he continued. "And so, it is without further ado that I ask you to step into my house of the bizarre, my museum of the extraordinary, my labyrinth of the grotesque. Ladies and gentlemen... *follow the doctor.*"

The crowd clapped again. Sigurdsson couldn't help raising an eyebrow at the choice of words.

Labyrinth of the grotesque

The group followed Mephisto, who led them forwards for a few paces before he stopped, gesturing for silence.

"Behind this curtain, ladies and gentlemen, is a creature that I captured myself, during a voyage across the Caspian Sea," he whispered reverently. "You have all heard tales, I'm sure, of the beautiful mermaids that dwell beneath the waves, luring sailors to a watery demise... and I won't deny that when I began the voyage, I hoped to myself encounter one of those seductive sirens. Imagine my horror when instead I found tangled in my fishing nets... a *merman!*"

He flung back the curtain to reveal a large fish tank, probably bought from an aquarium. Inside it was a creature that looked like it had crawled straight out of an HP Lovecraft novella. A long tail covered in scales was connected to a man's muscular torso, from which two arms extended, seeming to paw at the glass. But instead of a human head, the face that gazed out at them was more akin to that of a squid. Mephisto allowed their horrified stares to linger on it for only a few moments before he yanked the curtain back into place.

"Do not gaze upon it for too long, comrades, lest ye be driven *mad*!" he cackled, and Sigurdsson half expected to hear a clap of thunder soundtracking his words. Mephisto – Cronin – really seemed to be enjoying himself. His show was certainly impressive for such a low-budget affair; the creature in the tank had clearly been immobile, but even if it was only a sculpture of some sort, it was a disturbingly lifelike one.

"Let us make haste to the next exhibit!" Mephisto cried as he led them around the corner. "Here you will see a creature that has mercifully deceased, although the circumstances of its demise are a subject of much debate. Is this an alien traveller unable to survive in our atmosphere, captured and preserved by an enterprising scavenger? Or is this the mummified remains of an unwanted child, throttled and pickled by its own parents? It is hard to say which conclusion is the most disturbing… but now, you can judge for yourselves."

Once again, a curtain was tugged aside, this time unveiling a large glass bell jar, which was filled with yellowish liquid. Floating in the vinegary substance was another inanimate creature, this time barely larger than a baby. It was truly horrific, looking like something from HR Giger's worst nightmares, its multiple eyes seeming to stare accusingly at them from behind a tangle of knotted limbs, fangs and claws. Mephisto once again allowed them only the briefest glimpse before hurrying them onwards.

"They're waxworks," Mason whispered to Sigurdsson, before Mephisto's next soliloquy began.

The following couple of exhibits were a bearded lady, who again seemed mysteriously immobile, followed by an encaged 'serpent man'. This one was perfectly capable of motion, being essentially a bald bloke with lots of snake tattoos. But the crowd were getting into the spirit of the show, making exaggerated moans of shock and disgust at each revelation. The 'serpent man' delighted in wiggling his forked tongue at the crowd, and flashing his 'snake eye' contact lenses, and Mephisto let him milk it for a good few minutes before pulling the curtain back into place.

After several more entertaining showpieces, they reached the final exhibit, obscured behind a scarlet curtain draped across the entire back wall of the sports hall. Mephisto's voice dropped to a respectful whisper. "Now, ladies and gentlemen. I know your nerves must be frayed after a gruelling evening of shocks and surprises. But I would ask you to steel yourselves for one final revelation." Mephisto paused, as if even he needed to gather his composure. *He deserves an Oscar*, thought Sigurdsson.

"Behind this curtain is a woman I first encountered in the depths of the Malaysian jungle. I was able to entice her here only on the condition that I made her my highest paid act, and I must say it does not offend my sensibilities in the slightest to meet that stipulation. When you lay eyes on this exotic beauty, you may at first wonder what qualifies her to appear amongst this menagerie of oddities. But, if you look closely…"

Sigurdsson *was* looking closely. Behind Mephisto's head, the curtain had parted slightly, and a strange limb was wiggling into view. It curved left and right, almost like a snake… or a writhing tentacle. He realised that it was Lucy's arm, and the crowd laughed when she used it to wave at them. This distracted Mephisto from his speech, and the two of them engaged in an amusing panto routine, culminating in her snatching the top hat from his head and throwing it into the crowd.

When he finally realised what was going on, Mephisto gave his biggest grin of the evening, and turned once again to the crowd. "Ladies and gentlemen, I have been your humble host, Doctor Mephisto. And this is the one and only, the bedazzling, the mystifying, the notorious… *Octopus Girl!*"

The curtain dropped suddenly from the ceiling, revealing that a well-stocked bar had been installed along the back wall. Lucy Chen was standing behind it, smiling as she poured a pint.

The lights went up, and everyone clapped and cheered as Mephisto shouted above the applause.

"And now feel free to stay for a drink!"

Chen had to pose for lots of photos, as did the Serpent Man, who emerged from his cell to drink a few lagers and chat with the crowd. Cronin and his leprous servant also broke character, the latter revealing himself to be a teenager from a local drama group. They busied themselves removing the curtains and the other exhibits, being careful to conceal the sculptures as they did so, preserving their mystique for future outings.

By the time Cronin and his assistant joined them at the bar, Sigurdsson and Mason were already chatting with Chen and the Serpent Man, who had introduced himself as Curtis Reid.

"I know people probably ask you this all the time, but... does it hurt?" Mason asked him.

"Does what hurt?" Reid replied in a thick Gloucestershire accent.

"You know... the tongue thing?"

"Oh, right! I forget about it sometimes." He licked his lips theatrically. "Nahh, not really. The next thing people usually ask me is 'why did you do it?'"

"Hmm. I'm not going to ask you that."

"Oh?"

"I already know. You're a nutter."

Reid found this hilarious and laughed for a long time.

While they waited for his chuckling to subside, Chen addressed Sigurdsson. "How's your head?"

"Oh, yeah, fine," he replied sheepishly. "I didn't realise you'd be pulling pints here too."

"Got to make ends meet, somehow. Where's your friend?"

"I don't know. I thought she was going to be here. It was Daisy who recommended the show in the first place."

"Always nice to receive a glowing endorsement," chimed in Cronin, his voice completely different from his earlier southern-fried American twang; now he sounded mild-mannered and distinctly British. "I hope you two will spread the word about our little performance?"

"Of course," replied Mason. "Although you might be able to do something for us in return."

"Oh really? This sounds intriguing," replied Cronin with a smile, and suddenly he was Mephisto again, just for a second. Sigurdsson half-expected his bow tie to start spinning.

"We're detectives," she explained. "We're actually hoping to ask you a couple of questions about a missing person."

"I knew I'd seen you somewhere!" Cronin replied, snapping his fingers. "DI... Mason, isn't it? You visited the museum recently, with your daughter."

"I did. Holly had a great time. We both loved your waxworks."

"Shhh," Cronin replied, leaning in conspiratorially. "I don't want everyone to find out my secret! I'm pretty sure some of the people here thought they were real."

He was like Willy Wonka meets Doctor Frankenstein, decided Sigurdsson. It was very difficult not to warm to the eccentric curator.

"You make those things yourself?" Sigurdsson asked. Cronin shrugged modestly.

"A little hobby of mine. I get to put them to use in the museum, helping to tell the story of Salvation's history. And this little performance gives me a chance to show off my more... esoteric creations."

"They're very convincing."

Cronin bowed humbly. "Thank you. Now, you wanted to ask some questions?"

"Yes please. First, have you seen this man?" Once again, Sigurdsson extracted the photograph of David Lithgow, and passed it around the group. They each studied it, except for Chen, who had seen it once before. But they shook their heads, in turn.

"I might have seen them before, at the museum perhaps... certainly not recently," Cronin added.

"He left some notes behind," Sigurdsson continued, putting the picture away. "Pieces from a book he was writing, about the island. He makes mention of a cult… does that mean anything to anyone?"

He watched Chen's face carefully but couldn't read anything in her almond-shaped eyes. She shook her head, and Curtis Reid did too, shrugging. But Cronin's eyes sparkled as he replied.

"Oh, yes, the Church of the True Whisper – gosh, I haven't heard of them for quite some time. Did he say anything in particular about them?"

Sigurdsson and Mason exchanged glances.

"Nothing much," Sigurdsson replied carefully. "We're just trying to cover all the possibilities. Can you tell us more about them?"

"Cult is a bit of a strong word for them. They were more a sort of… hippie sect, I suppose. Very interested in spiritual healing. Started in the sixties and centred on the statue of Drogo being the focal point of the island's positive energies."

"Are they still in existence today?"

Cronin shook his head. "Not that I'm aware. There were rumours that they'd resurfaced, as something more sinister. Weird rituals, sacrifices, that sort of thing. All nonsense, of course."

He sipped his drink, which was a lavish cocktail with a paper parasol sticking out of it.

"Actually," he added pensively, "it might be worth looking up a gentleman named Ian Skelton. He was a journalist, working for one of those paranormal true story magazines that were quite popular for a while; you know, like *The Fortean Times*. He wrote a series of articles about Salvation. I remember he actually came out here to interview me."

Sigurdsson and Mason both reached for their notebooks to jot down the name.

"There's something else that crops up a lot in Lithgow's writing," Sigurdsson continued. "I think he was searching for an underground cave network of some sort. Is that something you've ever heard of?"

Cronin frowned thoughtfully. "You've heard the rumour about the poison gas, I assume?"

Sigurdsson nodded. "That the island was a nerve gas factory during the war? That the rabbits are the offspring of the test subjects?"

Cronin chuckled. "That's the one. I'm pretty sure Skelton wrote an article on that too, come to think of it. Anyway, one of the key components of that theory was that the recovering soldiers were secretly being tested on. An underground laboratory, directly beneath the convalescent home. Maybe that's what he was writing about."

"Let me guess… no one's ever found anything?"

Cronin nodded. "Just another fable… much as I love a spooky story." He flashed another devilish Mephisto smile and fiddled in his pocket. The bow tie rotated once again, and they all laughed.

As though attracted by the merriment, Edward Hardacre was suddenly stumbling towards them. The island's owner was grinning and ruddy-faced, clutching a tumbler of what looked like neat whisky.

"Hello, folks," he slurred at them as he approached. "Great show as usual, Bill. It's a shame it doesn't pull in the crowds anymore, eh?" He slapped Cronin on the back, too hard. The curator smiled graciously as Hardacre turned his attention to Chen.

"And always a pleasure to see you, Octopus Girl," he leered, winking. "I bet you know a few tricks with that tentacle, eh?"

Chen mirrored Cronin's tolerant expression. Sigurdsson felt repulsed; Hardacre's status as owner of the island clearly gave him the power to say whatever he felt like. Sigurdsson opened his mouth to say something, but Mason beat him to it.

"You look like you've had a good night, Mr Hardacre," she said icily.

He turned slowly to face her, swaying drunkenly. "Ahh, it's the Sheriff of Nottingham. I hope you're looking after my island, sweetheart?"

Mason raised an eyebrow. "I'm doing my job, if that's what you mean, *Ed*."

Hardacre laughed, jabbing a finger towards Sigurdsson without looking at him. "And what's he then? The backup?"

"Detective Sigurdsson is assisting with our investigation into the David Lithgow case," she replied coolly.

Hardacre hiccupped and coughed into his hand. "Is that the mysterious disappearing poet? I wish you'd all get a bloody move on. I want the house back."

"I know, Ed. You gave me until the tenth, remember?"

He gulped down the rest of his whisky and slammed the glass onto the bar. Then he grinned boozily at her. "Is that what I said? I don't remember. But I'm sure you were very persuasive."

He took a step closer to her. She backed away, calmly.

"I think your wife is looking for you, Ed," Sigurdsson interjected, stepping in between them. He pointed across the sports hall towards the double doors, where Hardacre's partner had just re-entered the room, presumably following a trip to the toilet.

But Hardacre didn't even turn to look. Instead he stared at Sigurdsson, squaring up to him.

"My *wife* isn't here; Joanna is my *mistress*. You know, for a detective, you aren't very perceptive."

Sigurdsson could smell the whisky on Hardacre's wheezing breath. His eyes narrowed as he replied. "You might own this island, but you don't own me. Remember that."

Hardacre's eyes blazed with momentary rage. Then he laughed and turned away. "Come on, this is supposed to be a *party*. Everyone needs to lighten up! Lucy, another Glenmorangie for me please."

He leant on the bar, mumbling compliments at her while she poured his drink and continued to smile politely. After a while he seemed to lose interest and lurched off towards the woman who was not his wife.

Mason and Sigurdsson watched him go.

"Let me guess. You're thinking 'arsehole'?" she commented.

"More specifically, I was wondering what 'Joanna' sees in him."

Mason rubbed a thumb against two extended figures. "Pound signs, I think."

"I wonder if that's true, though. I got the impression his finances were a bit of a mess."

"Not to mention his lungs, and his liver."

Thankfully, Hardacre and his partner left soon after that. The detectives spoke with Cronin and the others for a while longer, but no one knew anything more about the cult, or about any hidden underground labyrinths. After a while, Mason said she'd need to head home; Sigurdsson offered to walk her there, and she accepted.

They emerged into a still, silent darkness. The only sound was the faint lapping of the sea against the shore, and the low buzzing of the streetlights they walked past.

"So where are you staying?" she asked.

"The Marine View."

"Oh, Doug's place? He's a nice guy."

"Yeah."

They walked in silence for a while.

"So… do you have a babysitter now?" he asked awkwardly.

"Holly is staying at a friend's house tonight," Mason replied. "I wouldn't have been able to get someone to stay this late. She sleeps over there quite a lot, sadly."

"Oh, I see." He paused. "I'm sorry again about your mum."

She shrugged. "It's life. I just worry about Holly. First her dad, and now her nan."

"You never told me what happened with her dad," Sigurdsson said, not wanting to phrase it as a question, to push too hard. Mason shrugged again.

"Holly's dad… Thom… he was a bipolar sufferer too."

"Oh. God, that must have been hard for you."

"It was a lot of things at once. I was depressed, after she was born. Thom… wasn't able to support me. We both needed help that the other couldn't provide."

"Do you ever see him?" Sigurdsson asked. But Mason had fallen silent, and they didn't speak again until they reached her front door. It was still painted red, like Sigurdsson remembered it.

"Well… goodnight," he said. "I'll let you know if I make any progress tomorrow."

"You could… come in if you want?" she replied. "I would say 'for coffee' but I only have decaf these days."

He tried to read her expression, but he couldn't. Was he an old friend, who she was enjoying spending time with? Or something more? If it was the former, his sexual feelings for her made him feel rotten, false. Maybe he should decline. But instead, he found himself saying 'decaf sounds great', and following her inside.

The house was exactly as he remembered it. He followed her into the kitchen, where she gestured at some of Holly's artwork, specifically a carefully drawn picture of a smiling snowman, attached to the fridge with magnets.

"She drew that the other day. It's Olaf."

"I know who it is. I'm not *that* uncool you know."

Mason frowned at him. "You've seen *Frozen*?"

He blushed. "It was on TV the other day. I just wanted to know what all the fuss was about."

"In that case you'll know who Elsa and Anna are too. Holly drew that last week."

She pointed at another picture, again a near-perfect recreation of the Disney characters, the outlines drawn in felt pen and then partially coloured in, as though Holly had gotten bored halfway through and moved on to her next project.

"They're great," he said. But he was thinking about Lithgow's drawings, the pages stuck to the fridge back at the house on Smalley Lane. Leonard Spitt's eyes staring back at him from the photo on the kitchen door, seeming to peer out from Hell itself.

"I'm not sure why I invited you in, Chris," Mason said abruptly. That jerked him out of his thoughts, and he looked at her. She seemed suddenly vulnerable, leaning on her kitchen worktop. He imagined her cleaning it at the weekends, alone, like him.

"I…" he began and didn't know what to say. "I've missed you, Carin."

"It was so hard with Thom… It's like he sapped all of my love. Just… drained it away. I hate him for that."

"He would want you to move on though, surely?" Sigurdsson found himself saying. But she shook her head.

"He's dead, Chris. Thom killed himself after we left him. Holly doesn't know."

Sigurdsson opened his mouth, then closed it again. He had no words for her. He couldn't possibly relate to what she'd been through. He remembered the last time he had sat in this house, pouring out his troubles to her, about his brother's death, his anxiety attacks, his problems, him, him, him, him. He felt stupid, selfish.

"Anyway, that's why I've been acting like such a bitch. This whole Lithgow thing… it's bringing back bad memories. I see all that stuff, his 'troubled writer' shtick, his poor wife… I'm finding it hard to deal with."

Driven by a strange compulsion, Sigurdsson stepped towards her, and held her. She pulled back at first, but then leant forward to rest her head on his shoulder. He didn't pat her back, or stroke her hair, or try to kiss her. They just stood like that, for maybe a full minute.

Then she stepped away, turning to look out of the window. The mist had cleared briefly, and the bright orb of the moon was visible, like a coin flipped to decide their fate.

"Thanks, Chris," she said. "I should probably go to bed. You can… sleep here, if you like?"

He didn't know exactly what that meant. And he felt oddly ashamed of his desire for her.

And there were the pages. Hovering behind his thoughts. Seeming to call to him.

We never rest

"I should leave you in peace," he said. "But, Carin… please remember that you're a great policewoman, and a great mother. And a great friend."

She turned to face him, smiling. He thought she was about to shrug off his words, make one of her quippy remarks. But instead she simply said 'thanks'.

He left without saying another word, and for a long while the silence of Salvation's night seemed to belong to just the two of them.

It was only after a few minutes that he realised he had set out walking not towards the Marine View, but to the house on Smalley Lane.

Sixteen (The house)

Some notes on clandestine human testing

Nerve agents attack the nervous system of the human body, blocking the enzyme that enables the breakdown of acetylcholine in the synapse – in other words, they prevent muscles from relaxing.

Agents such as sarin will initially cause a runny nose, tightness in the chest, and constriction of the pupils. The victim will then begin to experience difficulty breathing, nausea, and uncontrollable salivation. Control over bodily functions will continue to deteriorate, and they will drool, weep, urinate, defecate, vomit, and experience chronic gastrointestinal pain. Blisters and the burning of the eyes and/or lungs may occur. If the process cannot be reversed via an antidote, a sufficiently potent agent will cause respiratory failure leading to death.

'The Novichok agents' were a series of nerve agents developed by the Soviet Union in the 1970s and 1980s. Allegedly they were the most deadly nerve agents ever created, and had the following objectives:

—   To be undetectable by NATO
—   To defeat NATO protective gear
—   To be safer to handle than previous agents

But the Soviet Union is not the only major global power to invest in the development of nerve toxins. The facility at Porton Down in the UK was the site of extensive trials of chemical weapons such as nitrogen mustard, anthrax, and botulinum toxin, as early as the 1940s. There is even a recorded death at the site following human trials, which were quickly abolished after the UK decided not to pursue a chemical warfare programme.

But perhaps the most infamous example of secret human testing is Project MKUltra. Rather than nerve agents, this programme explored the possibility of mind control via sensory deprivation, hypnosis, isolation, psychological torture, and the administration of hallucinogenic drugs.

The CIA-led initiative saw LSD administered to mental patients, prostitutes, prisoners, and drug addicts. The project began during a period of paranoia at the CIA, following the loss of the United States' nuclear monopoly, and at the height of the fear of Communism.

Sigurdsson stopped reading, pinching the bridge of his nose. The volume of data was starting to give him a headache. And he realised that a sound had been troubling him, a quiet but repetitive sound that had finally forced its way into his conscious brain. A creaking sound.

A glance at his watch told him that it was 04:23. Any minute, the first rays of sunlight would begin to penetrate the gloom outside the windows; but for now, it was dark, and he was tired, and alone. He had stayed up too late, scouring the words of a missing man for a clue to his whereabouts. Perhaps it was no surprise he was hearing things.

But there was the creak again, louder this time. Closer.

Like someone climbing up the stairs from the basement.

Slowly, he transferred the pages from his lap onto the seat beside him. As he stood, he reached for the torch in his pocket, testing its comforting weight. He took it out and walked cautiously towards the small hallway.

The sound had stopped. Had there even been a sound?

Maybe someone was standing right there, in the hall.

The bogeyman

Sigurdsson took a deep breath and yanked the door open. There was no one there. Nothing but the front door to his right, and the door to the basement on his left.

Silence, and darkness, on both sides.

He tested the front door, confirming that it was locked. There was no way someone else could be inside the house. But even so, he raised the torch like a club as he reached for the basement door's handle. He thought about someone standing on the other side, holding a butcher's knife.

A giant with a glassy-eyed stare

He didn't breathe.

Dragged into the basement, down to where he kept those terrible blue barrels

He turned the handle.

The door opened onto a wooden staircase. There was no one there.

He exhaled and reached for the light switch. The uneven steps led down into the same empty space he had already explored. He already knew there was nothing down there. But he couldn't let it beat him. He had vowed to himself five years earlier that he wouldn't be paralysed by fear, by his own mortality, any longer.

He descended the stairs, listening to the sound of his footfalls on the wood, trying to work out whether it matched the creaking noise he thought he'd heard earlier.

The basement itself was the same as the previous day. Floor covered in black tarpaulin. Smooth concrete walls. A single light bulb suspended from the ceiling like a hanged man.

He was suddenly gripped by the certainty that the labyrinth was *right under the house*. He clawed at the layers of tarpaulin, hauling them up from the floor, tearing away tape and pulling out staples as he did so. As he peeled back each layer, he expected to find a huge trapdoor, a concealed staircase leading down into the bowels of the island.

But instead, there was just a layer of packed, flattened earth. There were no dark patches to testify to the blood that this ground might once have consumed. Only featureless, uncaring dirt.

Sigurdsson laughed to himself. He laughed at the ridiculousness of his situation. He laughed until he forgot why he was laughing, and that just made it seem funnier.

Maybe you need some sleep, Chris

But when he emerged from the basement it was light outside, and he decided he might as well continue reading.

There is a bird trapped in the supermarket. I tell a shop assistant about it and he laughs and says it's been here for weeks, pecking at the bread. The other shoppers seem uninterested in its futile existence.

I walk down the bakery aisle, wondering if I will see the creature fly past. I realise that everything is slowing down, that my steps are dragging through the air like wings through tar. There is no one else in the shop. The assistant I spoke to has left. In front of me the tills have no cashiers, and there are no queues. The strip lights glow bright and the shop sparkles as clean as can be, but there are no customers. I realise I don't know what time it is, or how long I've been here. The windows are black, as though night has fallen outside while I've been wandering these aisles, up and down.

In my trolley everything is rotten. Flies are buzzing around the meat. I can see maggots crawling in the mushy bananas. As I walk, I am leaving a trail of stinking brown filth behind me, spoiling the see-your-own-reflection floor. The trolley is stacked with festering garbage. How long have I been pushing this thing around?

Someone is coming up the aisle towards me. I don't want them to see my disgusting cargo. It is embarrassing.

But my legs refuse to move. I can't turn away from the person either; my head is fixed in place, my eyelids jammed open. But still I can't make out the newcomer properly; they are vague, shifting like a watery reflection. As they approach, I see that they too are pushing a trolley.

Veins bulge in my arms as I try to haul my cargo around and get out of the way. It will cause a scene. It will be humiliating. This thing is so heavy. The flies are going crazy for the rancid lamb steaks.

It is a man coming towards me. He is smartly dressed in his work clothes, a nice suit and tie, a bit like mine actually. Why am I wearing these? Did I come straight from work? What is my job? His suit might be a little more expensive, or better pressed. His trolley is virtually empty but mine is piled high, and it fucking reeks to high heaven.

There is no sign of the bird. Maybe that has left too. Just the two of us, on this aisle.

I decide to play it cool and lean nonchalantly on the trolley's handle, as if I'm resting while deciding whether or not to buy some crumpets.

He walks past. Thank Christ. I didn't see whether he looked at me. But at least now we can go our separate ways. But as I turn I realise that he has stopped right behind me. He is looking at the scones on the other side of the aisle. Or at least he is pretending to look. The fucker. Maybe I should kill him. I could use the keys in my pocket, just plunge one right into his eyeball. If I had a breadknife I could slide it across his throat, part the flesh like silk.

No witnesses, because the place is empty. Empty and silent, except for the humming of the flies, and the drip-drip-drip of the rotten food in my trolley. The smell is making me feel nauseous.

The bird appears in a flutter of wings and lands on my trolley to peck at an open loaf of bread. My head hurts, a very deep and intense pain, like something is wrong with the inside of my brain. The dripping meat is like a hammer striking me in the skull. The buzzing insects are like a drill entering my ear canal.

I yawn unconvincingly and turn, slowly, casually... and he is staring straight at me.

He has my exact same face.

He is my doppelganger.

Behind me, the bird flies away.

Seventeen (The island)

At 08:12, Sigurdsson set out to jog back to the Marine View. He wanted to apologise to Doug and explain his absence the previous evening. But the old man wasn't in the little serving area; perhaps he was still in bed. So instead Sigurdsson headed to his own room, where he showered and changed and packed some clothes to take with him, as well as his laptop.

Doug appeared as he descended the stairs, emerging from the room behind the reception desk to bid him a good morning.

"I hope you don't mind me staying out last night," said Sigurdsson. "I should have called to let you know."

"Don't worry," Doug replied. "Did you visit your friend?"

Sigurdsson thought of the people he had met the previous day: Ed Hardacre, Doctor Mephisto, Serpent Man. A strange day indeed. Then he thought of Mason. "Yes. It was nice to see her."

"Good. Will you be wanting breakfast?"

He hadn't thought much about food, but now he realised he was starving. But it seemed too much of an imposition to expect the old man to cook for him after he'd just rolled in well after sunrise.

"No, that's okay. I need to head back out, I'm afraid. I might be out late again tonight too – is that okay?"

"Of course."

Doug must have thought he was some sort of ageing party animal.

Sigurdsson made his excuses and set out towards a row of shops on the promenade, where he bought a bacon roll from the only bakery he could find that was open and sat on a bench to eat it. He had never worked a night shift, but he imagined this was what it felt like; stumbling through the morning, his head a strange mixture of hyper-awareness and zombified disbelief that an entire night had passed with not one minute of sleep. Everything felt magnified and dulled at the same time. He watched the few people that passed him, the rabbits that hopped amongst the litter. One of them trotted hesitantly up to him, sniffed at his shoes and then darted away, as though detecting something wrong in his scent.

The things he had read the previous night seemed like part of a bad dream.

He had one more day left to make a tangible breakthrough, otherwise he would have to tell Brennan he was getting nowhere. If he was going to spend it in the house, he needed to be better prepared. He found a nearby supermarket, where he bought a blow-up bed and some cheap bedding, as well as more snacks. The food on the shelves seemed to squirm and writhe if he looked at it for too long, like there were maggots crawling on the boxes and jars. He blinked repeatedly, trying to will himself properly awake. The girl on the checkout gave him an odd look as she scanned his items.

He arrived at Smalley Lane and decided to call Brennan, as he had promised to do after two days. She answered almost immediately.

"Hi, Chris. I'm so glad you called; I've taken the day off work to make sure I didn't miss you."

"I'm afraid I don't have much of an update for you yet, Erina." He closed his eyes so that he didn't keep staring at the walls, where the words seemed to be slithering across the pages, like weird insects.

"Oh. Does that mean…?"

"No, no. I just need more time. There's a lot of material here in the house. I'm investigating a couple of leads."

"So, you're confident of making progress today?" She sounded desperate, pleading.

"I… can't say that I'm confident, Erina. But I will try."

She was silent for a while. Sigurdsson kept his eyes closed, patterns dancing across the inside of his eyelids like strange constellations.

"I understand," she said eventually. "I just… I feel so helpless. Should I be there, perhaps? Take more time off work? Would that help?"

"No." It came out more firmly than he intended, almost an instinctive response. He realised that he felt certain the island was dangerous, even though he couldn't name or explain the threat. "No, I think you should try to relax. I know that will be hard. But wait for my call tomorrow, and then we'll decide what to do next."

"Okay, Chris. I trust you."

He winced at the words. He only hoped he could do something to earn them.

After they said goodbye, he started to make himself a cup of coffee, but as he filled the kettle, he realised that it might well be the same appliance that Spitt had once used. Surely Hardacre would have replaced it, would have replaced every fixture or fitting in the house… but how could Sigurdsson be sure? For all he knew, he was using a kettle in which Spitt had once boiled human organs.

Sigurdsson went back to the supermarket and bought cutlery, plates, a saucepan. He would heat the water on the stove, just to be sure.

Eighteen (The house)

By the time Sigurdsson finally had his first sip of coffee, it was 10:36. He needed to hurry up.

The first thing he did was search online for Ian Skelton, the name Cronin had mentioned the previous night. Sure enough, he found a backlog of the journalist's work in a magazine called *Real Life Horror Stories*. Sigurdsson had to subscribe to the magazine in order to read the back issues online and was assured that he could look forward to a 'monthly compendium of the strange, the unexplained, and the deliciously deviant'. Doctor Mephisto would have approved. After trawling through a number of volumes, he managed to find the article he was looking for.

Healing and Sacrifice
(first published in 'Real Life Horror Stories' issue 276 1 March 2003)

No history of Salvation Island would be complete without a discussion of perhaps its most famous attraction, and certainly its most long established. The statue of Saint Drogo, which resides at the centre of the island next to the sixteenth-century chapel, has long been rumoured to possess magical powers. To this day, tourists visit the island to rub the statue's bronze foot and make a wish, which legend has it will be granted by the spirit of the island's adopted saint. In the 1950s there were three documented cases of healings following a visit to the island: a mute girl began to speak, a wheelchair-bound man was suddenly able to walk again, and a woman blind from birth was miraculously able to see.

Drogo himself is a strange character. Cast out by his own church to live in an annex after contracting a terrible (and unspecified) skin disorder, he was condemned to live out the remainder of his pious existence in enforced solitude, his unspeakable face hidden beneath a cowl. Such a tragic life might have spawned a spirit more inclined to vengeful hauntings than to benevolence, but Drogo has apparently transcended this legacy and continues to help people from beyond the grave. Among other things, he is the patron saint of sickness, insanity, broken bones, and 'those whom others find repulsive'.

It is perhaps no surprise that a religious group would choose the statue as the central focus of their adulation, and sure enough, in 1962 a group calling itself the Church of the True Whisper was officially formed. The chapel was still holding weekly Christian services at that time, and so the group was unable to secure its use for worship; instead they had to rent a space above a nearby public house and make a weekly 'pilgrimage' up the hill to gather around their chosen icon. Despite their unusual beliefs, they were well liked by the island dwellers, being friendly, peace-loving, and harmless. The group was named after its belief that God had spoken to a number of religious artefacts across the world, literally imbuing them with his spirit. Thus their worship was a celebration, and also a sort of quest, an attempt to seek out and understand the true word of God.

By the end of the decade, the 70s were ushering in a darker and more troubled time, and the group had disappeared, its members finding jobs on the mainland or drifting into other religious sects that perhaps offered more comfort in numbers. Thus the Church of the True Whisper would have become a minor footnote in the island's history and would scarcely merit a mention in this magazine.

But then the Church reappeared in 1988, in a darker guise altogether.

Sigurdsson's phone rang, interrupting him. It was Mason.

"Hi, Chris. Did you sleep okay?"

"Yes," he lied. "How about you?"

"Fine thanks." There was a stilted silence. "Are you back at the house?"

He stared at his computer screen, drawn to the words again.

Although no firm evidence has ever been obtained, several eyewitnesses claim to have observed bizarre rituals taking place in secret locations on the island, late at night.

"Chris?"

"What? Oh, sorry… I… sorry, Carin, I was just reading something."

"I thought so. You're still convinced you'll find a clue in his writing, aren't you?"

"I told Erina to give me three days to make a breakthrough. Today is my last day."

"And then… you're leaving?"

"Not if I can find something."

"Okay. I hope you do."

Did she mean for Brennan's sake, or because she didn't want him to go?

"I can't come and visit you because I'm holding the fort on my own today," she continued.

One witness, who we will refer to only as Ms X, says that she was out walking late at night when she observed a large flame burning in the middle of the old village ruins.

"Have you got enough food?"

When she approached to investigate, she saw several hooded figures gathered around a bonfire, chanting in a strange language.

"Chris?"

"Hmm? Oh, yes, I've been to the shop and stocked up, don't worry."

"Okay… Call me later and let me know how it's going."

"I will. I hope the island behaves itself for you today."

"Me too."

As Ms X watched, another hooded figure approached, carrying a long, sharpened branch. At the end of the makeshift skewer was an impaled rabbit.

"Anyway, I'll see you later, Chris."

It was only as the stake was held over the roaring blaze, and the chanting swelled to a crescendo, that Ms X realised that the rabbit was still alive, twitching and thrashing in agony as its fur caught fire.

She hung up. He realised, too late, that he hadn't said goodbye.

Other witnesses reported finding the words 'True Whisper', along with arcane symbols, daubed in blood on the ground in the woods. Another found a strange effigy 'resembling a slender man, made from rabbit bones bound together with grass'. But when they returned with a camera, the ghastly construction had vanished.

Who knows what dark god this new Church is seeking to appease? Perhaps they believe they have found the secret of Drogo's healing powers, and that blood sacrifice and pagan rituals can help them to channel his potent restorative magic. Or perhaps they are simply a group of hooded sadists, to be feared and reviled. Whatever their intention, the new Church of the True Whisper has managed to remain secretive and has joined the tangle of myths that surrounds Salvation Island.

As Cronin had mentioned, Skelton had written several articles about the island, all published at around the same time. Sigurdsson found one detailing Spitt's murders in graphic detail. There was nothing he didn't already know, but the specifics still made his flesh crawl. The article also included a photograph of the killer, which appeared to be the same picture Lithgow had pinned to the back of the kitchen door. Sigurdsson didn't linger on the image, but he did wonder for a moment why the picture hadn't been given more prominence in Lithgow's 'command centre'; after all, Spitt was the centrepiece of his book. Perhaps Lithgow himself had moved it, unable to work beneath that terrible, empty stare; those cold eyes, like balls of glass.

Another article by Skelton caught his eye, this time recounting the circumstances of the alleged bombing of Salvation.

Midnight Massacre
(first published in 'Real Life Horror Stories' issue 278 1 May 2003)

Salvation Island was attacked in a Nazi bombing raid on 4 August 1940. The convalescent home housed one hundred and forty patients at the time, and the island was home to a further four hundred and ninety-one people, all living in the nearby village.

Every single soul was killed under a hail of bombs that demolished most of the buildings and left the island a charred, smouldering ruin. It was reported as a great wartime tragedy, an appalling example of the civilian casualties that Britain suffered during the Blitz. The island remained dead and desolate for sixteen years, until it was purchased and rebuilt by Thomas Hardacre, reimagined as a seaside resort town.

But I am compelled to ask: why would the Germans choose to destroy a target so insignificant, and so far from the mainland? Were the deaths of a few wounded, shell-shocked soldiers really worth the expenditure of so much effort and ammunition, in such a carefully co-ordinated attack?

If you have heard of Salvation you have doubtless also heard of its famed rabbit population, the creatures running wild on a land mass that has no natural predators. Some believe that the animals are the descendants of a group of test subjects, brought to the island for use in clandestine experimentation with poison gas and nerve toxins. If the Nazis had obtained intelligence regarding such a secret weapons development programme, it would certainly explain the strategic value of a bombing attack.

However, I have unearthed a more disturbing theory. My source, close to the UK military, claims that the attack on Salvation was not perpetrated by the Nazi Luftwaffe at all.

It was instead carried out by our own government.

The reason for this shocking cover-up was that a particular strain of chemical agent being developed on the island had yielded unexpected results, and the dangerous test subjects had escaped. Their eradication was treated as a top priority – too important for the lives of a few island dwellers to matter.

If at this point you are anticipating a silly story about giant, flesh-eating rabbits, please read on. The truth, I'm afraid, is far worse.

The toxin, administered in gaseous form and designed for use as a potent airborne poison, was being tested not only on rabbits in the laboratory, but also on some of the human population of the convalescent home. Soldiers with severe injuries and mental disorders were being reported as deceased but were in fact being used to gather experimental data on the effects of the new chemical weapon.

My source, who claims to have worked in the programme, named 'Operation Dark Harvest', described the night of the escape.

'They'd had to imprison the latest batch – that's what we called them, the small groups of soldiers that were selected for trials of the most promising compounds – because exposure to the gas had caused them to become highly aggressive. One of the orderlies had already been badly bitten by a patient that had previously been in a catatonic state. Other than the control specimen – I'm sorry, I'm so sorry for what I did, and that I don't even know the poor man's name – the rest of the batch became increasingly agitated while in isolation, some of them even starting to exhibit disturbing autophagous tendencies. We think that's how the escape occurred, that one of the staff opened the cell to assist a man that was literally chewing off his own hand… somehow they triggered all five cell doors to open by mistake, and the specimens – the soldiers – escaped into the tunnels.'

Tunnels.

By the time we were alerted, at least three of them had reached the village. We hadn't prepared for this – the local team were scientists, not security personnel. They had followed a trail of carnage from house to house and had even managed to subdue one of the escapees while he… they said he was knelt beside a woman, devouring her insides, smiling. But the others had escaped into the woods… We decided that we couldn't afford a scandal on this scale. You've got to remember that this was wartime

Britain — every single ounce of focus and effort was directed towards battling Hitler. An incident like this… had to be contained. Suppressed.' Here my source broke down in tears. *'So we ordered the air strike.'*

The article was lurid and dramatised, much more concerned with entertaining the magazine's readership than with presenting an accurate account. But even if the tale was nothing more than a hack's concoction, the important thing was not whether it was true — it was simply whether David Lithgow had *believed* that it was. And what that belief had led him to do next.

I'm onto something, Erina

The words were starting to dance on the computer screen. Sigurdsson rubbed at his eyes and closed the laptop, deciding to switch to reading Lithgow's writing again; at least that was in hard copy form, and might be less of a strain. He moved from the couch to the table and started to work through another as-yet-unsorted pile of documents.

He read for hours, forgetting to eat. He read extracts from scientific journals and historical newsletters. He read detailed accounts of what was believed to have happened on the nights of Spitt's six murders. He read scribbled notes that barely made sense. He read fragments of poetry. He found printouts of all three of the Ian Skelton articles he had already read and read them again. He viewed top-down diagrams of cult rituals, detailing the position and line of sight of the alleged witnesses. His eyes ached. His brain shrieked at him to get some sleep. Eventually, as daylight was beginning to fade, he decided that he might be better equipped to tackle another late stint if he acquiesced.

He inflated the blow-up bed in the front room and made a pillow out of his spare clothes. He opened a pre-packed sandwich and poured a glass of water and slumped into the couch to eat and drink. Then he picked up a sheet of paper that had the single word DESCENT printed on one side, and rows of typewritten text on the other. He would read this, whatever it was, and then he would take a brief 'power nap'.

He flipped over the page.

I have stopped taking my medication. I know this is a gamble and that my doctors and friends would advise against it. They like this neutered, pacified shadow that the pills have made of me. But I know that my emotions are me, and I am them, and that we need each other if we are going to create anything, ever again. And so, it is wilfully that I open the portal in my head, revealing that dark abyss and the tantalising promise within its shifting depths. I step inside it with the fear and determination of Theseus stepping across the threshold of the labyrinth.

It is a dark place, and no mistake. Torches line the walls, but their flames flicker and sputter like ailing heartbeats, and the gloom is too strong for them. The first trick of the labyrinth is that it is not a labyrinth at all, at least not at the beginning: only this long, straight corridor, aiming to test my resolve far more than my navigational skills. I fancy that pairs of malignant eyes observe me from cracks and crevices in the walls as I traverse its length. How far has it been now: miles, kilometres, leagues, lifetimes? The thread between my fingers leads back into the distant darkness like a single, fading memory. My sword feels heavy in my other hand, but not with reassuring weight — heavy instead with dread, and regret, and expectation.

When I reach the first intersection, I almost sink to my knees and weep with relief. I feel like I have grown old and died and been reborn a thousand times since I set out down that accursed passage. But those lifetimes all have the same inevitable outcome, the illusion of all my choices funnelling me inexorably to this same crossroads. I know it is not a decision, not really. All three of the gaping black passageways that face me, like screaming mouths, will only lead me deeper

into

Zero (Hell)

*W*here it is hot, very hot now. I've been aware of the downward incline for miles; only very slight, but enough to have taken me deep beneath the surface after so many hours of walking. The oppressive heat of the earth envelops me. I begin to wonder if the dreaded Minotaur is nothing more than this stifling warmth, his infamous roar the sound of blood rushing in my ears as it starts to boil. I press on. Perhaps there is no Minotaur at all. Perhaps instead a grand prize awaits me at the centre of this accursed place. Wealth. Immortality. The True Word of God.

Or maybe she is there, waiting for me. She was always the architect of my pain.

And besides, of course there is a Minotaur. I can feel his presence at every turn, sense him hanging behind me in the shadows that obliterate the memory of my path, swallowing my past like wriggling morsels in a great gaping throat. I picture the muscular figure with the head of a bull that is depicted in children's books, movies, websites, and try to reconcile it with the shuffling, hesitant footsteps at my back. I imagine that same creature made gaunt, sallow, desperate, emaciated by lack of nourishment. Salivating at the thought of a feast when I finally collapse, my organs warm and succulent in its mouth.

I imagine Spitt's victims, a sad procession shambling behind me, leaning on each other for support. Some carry their severed appendages, while others argue over limbs stitched to the wrong bodies, like the Graeae.

Or maybe it's Anax, padding faithfully behind me. Perhaps the Minotaur is the hunted, not the hunter; me and my faithful hound, pursuing the baleful creature deeper into its lair. Maybe Anax, bewildered by the heat, believes I am his master, Edward Hardacre.

When he realises that I am in fact merely Chris Sigurdsson, the beast's footsteps will quicken, his massive bulk will crash into me from behind and I'll feel his teeth crunch through my neck.

Perhaps I am the Minotaur. Those whores think they can outsmart me, that I won't solve the puzzle. I'll catch them, and I'll gut them. I'll follow them to the centre of the earth if I have to. My butcher's knife is sharp, keenly sharp, keen to stab and slice and rend and saw and perhaps Marcus is there, waiting for me. He was always the architect of my pain. No, it wasn't his fault. A terrible accident. I used to think of him and panic, crushing panic, oppressive heat and walls closing in around me like this labyrinth, inescapable and choking and immense.

But now I am calm, serene, like the sea, softly undulating behind the fog.

Serene, as the dog looms up in front of me and I whip the blade across its throat and blood spurts out into my face, dark blood, thick and black like tar, black tendrils that curl out of the shadows and drag me towards them, absorbing me into their soothing folds, like the sea, and I'm fallen into the sea and sinking so peacefully like a stone, barely making a ripple, like a single tear

D

r

o

p

Nineteen (The house)

Music was playing. It was muffled and indistinct. How could music be playing in this dark place, deep underground? Because this dark place was not underground. It was the blackness inside his eyes. He opened them.

The darkness remained.

The music was the sound of a phone ringing. His phone ringing.

Sigurdsson fumbled towards the noise and lifted the handset to his ear.

"Hello," he mumbled. There was no answer, because he'd already missed the call. The screen told him that it had been Priya.

He scrambled onto his knees, using the light from the phone to illuminate his surroundings, which seemed to be featureless. As he stood and turned, confused, the light revealed some wooden stairs.

He was in the basement.

What the…

Hell?

He hauled himself groggily up the steps and out into the hallway. Light was spilling into the house through the windows. How long had he…

The phone rang again.

"Hello," he repeated.

"Sigs, for God's sake, I've been trying to call you all morning!" It was Priya. "Are you okay?"

He staggered into the front room. It was just as he had left it. The blow-up bed was there, the piece of paper bearing the word DESCENT lying next to it on the floor, along with the remnants of his sandwich wrapper.

"I… Hi, Pri. Yes, I'm fine. I… think I overslept, maybe."

He grabbed the piece of paper, his eyes scanning down the printed text.

'All three of the gaping, black passageways that face me, like screaming mouths, will only lead me deeper into hell' were the last words on the page.

"Sigs, you called me last night. I was asleep. You left me a really weird message. I was worried sick."

He sensed something else was out of place. His gaze flicked around the room, his mind still reeling and disoriented. "I… did I? I don't remember… are you sure?"

"I can play it for you if you like. You were babbling all sorts of rubbish, about slit throats, about finding the Word of God, about the Minotaur being the true killer… were you drunk?"

Leonard Spitt's picture was staring at him from the kitchen door. It had somehow moved from one side of the wood to the other. It was watching him. If it didn't look so lifeless, the smile might almost have been a mocking sneer.

His mind raced. Had he sleepwalked, somehow? Called Priya, moved the picture, ended up sleeping down in the basement? The prospect chilled him. He felt nauseous, and somehow violated.

Unless…

"I wasn't drunk, Pri. I think maybe I… was half asleep, or something. I'm sorry to have scared you."

There was someone else there. Someone messing with him, moving the picture, dragging him into the basement while he slept.

"Look, Sigs, I'm worried about you. If this case is getting to you… just remember you don't owe this woman anything. I know you have history there…"

What, and leaving a message for his assistant, impersonating his voice? *Get a grip, Chris!*

"I'm fine, Pri. I told Brennan I would spend three days trying to find a lead."

"And have you?"

"Erm… is it… Sunday?"

She sighed down the phone. "Yes, Sigs."

"Then I've failed. But there's so much material here, Pri. I'm convinced that it will lead us to Lithgow."

"You mean to Lithgow's body?"

He opened his mouth, then said nothing. He realised he didn't know. Mason was convinced that Lithgow was dead, a suicidal bipolar sufferer like her own husband had been, who had tragically committed suicide during a period of intense stress.

But to Sigurdsson, Lithgow seemed like a man with a purpose. Obsessed. Not someone on the verge of giving up.

"Chris?"

"Priya, just let me gather my thoughts, okay? I haven't been sleeping well, since I came here. It's my own fault. I must have crashed out last night." He realised that his gaze had been drawn to Spitt's picture once again. "Let me figure out what I'm going to do, and I'll let you know. Is that okay?"

"Of course, Sigs. You're the boss." She sounded slightly scolded. He felt guilty.

"How's Casper doing?" he said, trying to change the subject.

"He tasted great with ketchup and chips," she replied, and hung up.

He smiled, then grimaced as a jolt of pain lanced through his skull. Great. A splitting headache was just what he needed.

As he sank into the couch, still clutching the DESCENT note, he realised that he had other missed calls on his phone. Four were from Priya, but two were from Mason. He called Mason back, and she answered almost immediately.

"Hi, Carin. Listen, I–"

"Chris, sorry, I can't talk now – did you get my voicemail?"

"I, er, haven't listened to it yet." He hadn't even noticed that she'd left one. He needed some coffee.

"We found a body this morning."

The words almost didn't register. "What?"

"Hardacre did, to be precise. He was walking that bloody dog, near the amusement park. Spotted her through the fence.

A middle-aged woman, dumped out in the wasteland. She had knife wounds all over her, like… Jesus, Chris, it was like she'd been tortured. We think maybe she escaped, but then collapsed before she could reach help. Hardacre said the fucking rabbits were crawling all over her."

Sigurdsson played the words back in his head, and a nagging suspicion immediately surfaced. "What did she look like?"

"Short, a little stocky, dyed blonde hair. Her face is a fucking mess and she has no ID, so identifying her won't be easy."

"What was she wearing?"

Mason paused. "Chris, I shouldn't really be telling you any of this, to be honest. It doesn't have any bearing on your case."

"Unless the killer is the same person who murdered David Lithgow."

She made a scoffing noise. "And is that what you're saying now? That he was murdered? Based on what?"

"Just tell me what she was wearing."

"Combat pants, a T-shirt, an orange puffer jacket. All covered in blood."

Sigurdsson's jaw clenched, grimly. His hunch had been right.

You can come back tomorrow and do all the trespassing you want, when I'm not here

"I knew her, Carin."

"What?"

"Remember I told you I was in the Cloak and Dagger on Wednesday? I was with someone I'd bumped into while I was out running. Her name was Daisy. I don't know her surname. She was an urban explorer, and she'd been about to go…" He paused as he realised that Daisy might have found something during her explorations. Something that had gotten her killed. "She was heading into the amusement park."

"Could you come to the hospital to make the identification?"

"Of course."

"I'll send Mitchell to pick you up. Are you at the Marine View?"

"No. I… stayed at the house last night."

Silence. "Jesus, Chris. You *slept* there?"

"I'm just trying to solve this thing. And you can't tell me now that there's nothing to solve. Even if you don't believe Lithgow was one of the victims; either way, you've got a killer on your island again, Carin."

"I know. And I'll fucking catch him. Now sit tight, and Mitchell will be there in five minutes."

He hung up and hurried upstairs to clean his teeth and splash water on his face. As he came back down the stairs, he once again locked eyes with Leonard Spitt, and felt a sudden urge to rip the picture off the door and tear it into pieces. But somehow that seemed like a desecration of David Lithgow's last work; and besides, Spitt hadn't murdered Daisy, or Lithgow. Spitt was long dead.

Sigurdsson went outside to wait for Mitchell.

Mason's deputy pulled up minutes later. He didn't wave or signal to Sigurdsson; the thick slab of a sergeant sat in the driver's seat of the idling squad car, waiting for the detective to climb in. Sigurdsson obliged, saying hello as he clambered into the passenger seat. Mitchell grunted, and set off.

"You know, I don't even know your first name," Sigurdsson said after a few minutes of weaving through narrow, potholed roads.

"Mitchell's fine," the burly policeman replied after a long silence.

Sigurdsson looked at the scar that emerged from the sergeant's shirt collar and climbed all the way to the cleft in his chin. Mitchell had once saved his life. That case, those incidents, seemed like something that had happened to another person, in another universe; a universe to which he had been summoned, once again.

Whenever he visited Salvation, people died.

"I never said thank you."

Mitchell continued to stare straight ahead, his face rigid and expressionless. He gave a slight shrug.

"Don't worry about it."

They didn't speak again. The island glided past outside, grey and desolate, mimicking their silence.

Twenty (The hospital)

When they arrived at the hospital, Sigurdsson recognised the Victorian building; it looked even more weather-beaten than when he'd last seen it, like a cliff face being slowly eroded by the sea breeze. They headed inside. Nothing seemed to have been updated or refurbished since Sigurdsson's last visit; everything was the same, but five years older. Like him. He followed Mitchell to the mortuary, down corridors painted the colour of wet sand.

Mason was standing in one corner, speaking with a tall, slim, black man. Between them, a shape lay beneath a plastic sheet on a gurney. Sigurdsson and Mitchell walked over to join them. The tall man was the new pathologist, a fresh-faced and nervy character who stammered and fidgeted when he spoke. Mason explained who Sigurdsson was, and that he was here to preliminarily identify the body, and the pathologist introduced himself as Greg Harrison, newly assigned to the hospital. After their pleasantries had concluded, a silence settled on them, like a shared secret. Sigurdsson watched Harrison's long, spidery fingers as they drummed against each other.

"Okay, I suppose we should get this over with," the pathologist said eventually, and reached down to pull back the sheet.

Sigurdsson remembered the last time he had been there. He had stood facing a similar gurney, watched as a similar sheet was peeled away. Back then he had stared down into an unfamiliar face, the face of a man whose years of spite and debauchery had seemed to somehow choke him from within. This time, he looked down into a face he had been speaking to only three days earlier. On Thursday night, it had been amiable, mischievous, playful. Now it was a mangled ruin.

A deep knife wound began at one corner of Daisy's forehead, sliced through her left eye, and opened her face all the way to her mouth. If she had survived she would have been horribly scarred, and certainly half-blinded. There was severe bruising around her other eye, and her nose looked badly swollen, possibly broken. Her mouth was open, and he could see that some teeth were missing.

He was reminded, for a horrible moment, of Doctor Mephisto's grisly waxwork creations. Daisy's battered face, her body, this whole terrible situation, didn't seem real.

But it was.

"It's her," he whispered, sadness and anger shaking his voice.

Harrison nodded and replaced the sheet.

"Thanks, Chris," Mason said. "This will help us track her down and get some family to come and formally ID her. Can I ask you some questions about her?"

Sigurdsson nodded dumbly, imagining someone striking and slashing at Daisy's face as she screamed and cowered.

No, not someone. For some reason, when he imagined the killer, he thought only of Leonard Spitt.

"Is there a room we could use, Doctor Harrison?" Mason asked.

"Oh, yes, of course. This way," the pathologist replied nervously, ushering them towards a small corner office. He closed the door on them gently, as if they were grieving relatives.

"Pretty bad, eh?" Mason asked him.

He nodded. "She was a sweet lady. Harmless, a bit eccentric. I can't believe this has happened."

"Harrison said she has several broken ribs, a broken arm, multiple stab wounds all over her body."

"Was she in any condition to have escaped? Or was she just dumped there?"

"He says that livor mortis suggests she died where she was found. Which means she maybe tried to run but didn't make it. The cause of death was blood loss rather than one specific injury."

"Was there a lot of blood at the site?"

"Enough for her to have bled out there, but not enough to suggest that's where the attacks took place. But she could have been mutilated, then dumped while still alive, and bled to death on the spot."

"But no footprints you can follow?"

"The earth's too dry."

"I'd like to go and take a look."

Mason seemed not to hear him. "Tell me what happened on Thursday," she said, taking out her notepad.

"I'd been in the house for a while after you left. I wasn't getting anywhere with Lithgow's writing, so I went for a run to clear my head. I ended up outside the amusement park. I saw a light moving about on the other side of the fence, a torch. It seemed odd, so I investigated. It turned out to be an urban explorer. I told her it was dangerous."

What did you stumble onto, Daisy?

"And then you… went to the pub?"

"I was trying to convince her not to go poking around in an abandoned theme park in the middle of the night. She agreed to go for some food and a drink instead. That's where I met Lucy Chen, and heard about Mephisto's show."

"And then what happened?"

"I walked Daisy home to her hotel after a few drinks. It was maybe about eleven. I left her on the doorstep and then went back to my guest house."

"Where was she staying?"

"A little B&B called the Belvedere."

"So you didn't go inside with her?"

He frowned at her. "Carin, if I didn't know better, I'd think you were interrogating me."

Or maybe a little jealous

"I'm just trying to work out her movements, Chris. You might be the last person who saw her alive."

"Of course. Well, the answer is no – I didn't go inside."

"And you haven't spoken to her since?"

He shook his head. Then a horrible thought occurred to him. "She was really keen on watching Mephisto's show. It was she who recommended it to me. But she wasn't there on Friday night. Do you think… maybe she was kidnapped earlier that day, and was held and tortured since then?"

Close to forty-eight hours

"Did she tell you what else she was doing on Friday?"

"She was planning on going back to the amusement park, during the day. Maybe she found something. We should search it."

Mason nodded.

"We've already searched the immediate scene and found nothing. I've got more officers coming from the mainland to help with a wider search of the entire park this afternoon. But I'll send Mitchell to take you for a look around now, if you like. I'd better get busy trying to trace her family. At least now I know her name – or the name she gave you."

"She said she was active on social media, uploading videos to YouTube. You could start with that."

"Okay, thanks."

"Who have you got securing the site?"

"I had to drag Clive out of bed. That's it, remember? I don't have anyone else. It's impossible with a team this size."

"How many extra men are you getting?"

"Two. I'll be briefing them later."

"Can't you get more?"

"I'll let you try arguing with Rampling, shall I?" she replied crossly, presumably referring to her new commanding officer.

"Sorry. I hope I can at least help you. I'll go with Mitchell right now and take a look at the scene."

He rose and headed for the door.

"Chris," she said as he reached for the handle. "It's just strange you didn't mention her, that's all. If… something happened between you two, it would be better to tell me. If it comes out later, it won't look good for you."

He turned to look at her. He knew he should feel angry; angry that she didn't trust him, that she was essentially accusing him of hampering a murder investigation. But instead he only felt sad. "Nothing happened, Carin. She was a funny, nice person who I had a drink with. And now some despicable bastard has murdered her."

She held his gaze, and then nodded, as though she had made up her mind to trust him. "Okay. I'm sorry. And I really do appreciate your help. Especially as I still think this has nothing to do with Lithgow's disappearance."

Sigurdsson forced a smile. "Just think of me as an unpaid intern."

She smiled back and followed him out of the little office. But they both knew something strange had passed between them, like a dark cloud across the sun.

Minutes later, he was back in Mitchell's squad car, heading once again towards the amusement park.

Twenty-one (The amusement park)

They parked on the promenade and climbed through the fence. The mist was thin today, otherwise there was no way Hardacre would have spotted the body from this distance. They could see the blue shape of the tent that had been erected over the scene and headed towards it. Sitting outside it was Mason's other full-time officer, who Sigurdsson had never met. Mitchell wandered over to the small, grey-haired policeman, explaining what they were there to do. Clive nodded and extended a hand to Sigurdsson, introducing himself. He was probably nearing sixty but looked compact and capable. He also looked as tired as Sigurdsson felt.

"You helped us with a case once before," Clive said in a Northern Irish accent, more as a statement than a question.

"I did," Sigurdsson replied. "I hope I can do it again. Do you mind if I take a quick look in there?"

Clive shrugged. "If the boss trusts you, I trust you." He led the way into the tent.

There was nothing to see except a sad patch of earth, and a dark stain that marked the end of Daisy's life. The police don't draw chalk outlines in real life, so Sigurdsson didn't know exactly where she had been found, but he could imagine the grisly scene. After a while he felt rage boiling inside him and stepped back outside. Wordlessly, he and Mitchell headed towards the looming shape of the Ferris wheel.

The park, unsurprisingly, had been called Bunnyland. Most of the attractions were rabbit-themed, or at least had grinning cartoon bunnies painted all over them. The carousel had rabbits instead of horses. The caterpillar ride had been modified with long ears and a fluffy tail. Even the ghost train was decorated with zombie rabbits, alongside the usual vampires and werewolves, and of course the giant leering skeleton that had frightened him on Thursday night.

Mitchell stopped when he reached the main thoroughfare, where Sigurdsson and Daisy had first met in the dark. Now in the daylight the street looked dusty and litter-strewn. Rabbits were everywhere, peering at them from the holes they had dug all over the rundown site.

"I'll take left, you take right?" Sigurdsson suggested. The proper search would come later, of course; Mason and her reinforcements would have to comb every inch of ground in meticulous detail. This was about looking for anything big and obvious.

Like the entrance to a secret underground labyrinth

Mitchell grunted his agreement.

"How do we keep in touch?" Sigurdsson asked.

Mitchell unclipped a two-way radio from his duty belt and handed it to him. Then he turned and headed without a word towards the gift shop.

Sigurdsson looked up at the skeleton and decided to get the ghost train over with first. He pulled out his torch and climbed carefully up the rotting wooden steps that led into the ride. The two-person carts were styled to look like vampire rabbits, with passengers sitting right inside their fanged mouths; they would have trundled past, stopping briefly to admit another pair of giggling children or reluctant parents, perhaps even expecting the visitors to scramble in while they were still moving. Either way, now the carts were motionless, covered in rust and mould.

Sigurdsson followed the track, pushing open the sagging wooden doors and stepping inside the ride itself. He switched on his torch, illuminating wooden partition walls covered with peeling black paint. After a few metres, the tracks turned sharply to the right, leading deeper into the ride. A fluorescent plastic skeleton had once hung on the wall here, but now it lay across the tracks as if it had been mowed down by a train. The skull grinned up at Sigurdsson as he stepped gingerly past.

The stink of mould and mildew grew stronger as he turned the corner, a sickly fetor that made him cough and gag. He tugged his shirt up over his nostrils and continued, holding the torch beside his head with his other hand. He realised he had ignored all the advice he had given to Daisy on Wednesday evening: he had no breathing filter, no special equipment, not even appropriate footwear. But he pressed on, ignoring the garishly painted monster on the wall to his left, which he vaguely remembered as being called a 'manticore' from his gaming days. The low budget horrors continued as he followed the track in a clockwise circle.

A prison cell to his right held a dummy pressed up against the bars, staring out at him with a disturbingly inane smile on its face.

Vacuous, like Spitt.

To his left was an effigy of Cerberus, the three-headed guardian of Hades. It seemed he was descending into Hell via Greek mythology, once again.

Maybe the Minotaur will be waiting for you, at the centre

A dummy was attached to the wall by some sort of mechanism that had presumably dropped it towards the carts as they went past. It was made up to look like Sadako from *The Ring*, her long black hair perhaps tickling the revellers as they passed by, screaming. A procession of shrieks, some delighted and some truly terrified, round and round and round, until Bunnyland had one day ground to a halt. He prodded Sadako carefully, as if he expected her to suddenly lunge at him, but the dummy felt lifeless, damp and filthy.

The track led him onwards, and he noticed a door marked 'staff only' concealed behind a slobbering gargoyle. He tried it and found it was unlocked, opening into another corridor that created an extra loop on top of the main circuit. This area housed a small staff room in its centre, with a couple of dead CCTV monitors, and was clearly where broken or unwanted parts and models were stored. In one corner was a hideous ogre whose arm seemed to have been snapped off. In another was a heap of humanoid figures.

Sigurdsson shone his torch at them, and saw that they were zombies, all clawed hands and rotting flesh. None of the models could hold a candle to Doctor Mephisto's elaborate creations, but nevertheless the place was beginning to freak him out.

The pile moved. For a few terrible moments, he thought the B-movie creatures were rising from their sleep, ravaged faces turning to snarl and gnash their teeth at him.

Then several rabbits shot out from under the pile, scampering in terror into other hiding places. Within seconds, they had disappeared.

So many things hidden in the shadows, watching.

He finished his circuit as meticulously as he could but was relieved when he emerged once again into daylight and took a deep breath of the fresh air. The skeleton grinned down at him as if amused by his fruitless search. He gave it a two-fingered salute, and glanced across the path, where another sign caught his eye.

AMUSEMENT ARCADE

The words were inside a speech bubble, emerging from a bright green rabbit's mouth; it had pound signs instead of pupils in its eyes, and was giving a thumbs-up gesture. Almost directly beneath it, one of the shutters had been removed, and the glass of the automatic doors had been smashed to allow access. He doubted Daisy would have done that herself, but she might have found it a tempting invitation to explore.

He crossed the street and ducked inside, avoiding the jagged edges of the broken pane.

When he was young and struggling to cope during his troubled childhood, Sigurdsson had been an avid gamer. He had shut himself away in his room and spent hours with his ZX Spectrum, then his Nintendo Entertainment System, then his Sega Megadrive, as he worked his way through the most popular home systems of the time. The tiny screen of his bedroom TV had been a window into another world, a world of garish colour, surreal sights and sounds, fun and excitement and blissful *escape*. There had been very few holidays in the Sigurdsson household, and so he'd had little opportunity to play actual *arcade* games until he was much older, but he'd still been fascinated by them; he'd voraciously devoured gaming magazines and watched every episode of programmes like *GamesMaster*, so he knew all about the most popular arcade machines and had relished any chance to try his hand at *Street Fighter* or *Gauntlet* or *R-Type*. Of course, some of these classic titles had found their way onto his home consoles, but he knew they were always a watered-down, diluted, B-grade version. It was only towards the end of the 90s that Nintendo and Sony had developed machines powerful enough to make their arcade counterparts obsolete, and amusement arcades began their slow demise. By the mid-2000s, places like this were little more than an anachronism, a home for faddish gimmicks like dancing stages or ridiculous life-sized shotguns.

And so, he entered the large, open-plan interior with a strangely mixed feeling: the wide-eyed, childish glee of a ten-year-old Chris Sigurdsson – stepping into an amusement arcade for the first time, almost exploding with excitement at the fun he would have until his supply of ten-pence pieces ran out – merged with jaded disappointment as he surveyed the rows of uninspiring fruit machines, cynical grabber games, and tedious modern shooters.

But as he walked slowly along the banks of machines, some vandalised, others seemingly untouched, he still saw things that brought a smile of nostalgia to his face. A 'whack-a-mole' game, rebranded of course as 'bash-a-bunny', the padded mallet attached by a chain to the chunky game console. A 'penny falls' machine that contained an ancient one-pound note as its tantalising special prize. A Namco *Point Blank* game cabinet, with one of the guns missing. He didn't know what amused him more: the idea of firing it up so that he could blast holes in an array of cardboard criminals, bouncing balls and creepy uncles, or the idea that a vandal somewhere thought he looked cool carrying around a bright pink plastic gun.

But the dead screens and the stench of mould reminded him that he wasn't there to play games and reminisce. He was there to help catch a killer.

After turning a few corners, he stopped briefly at one of those fortune-telling machines, a transparent plastic box housing a sinister clown surrounded by plastic baubles, each containing a printed statement of the player's destiny. The grinning horror was no less terrifying than some of the things he had seen inside the ghost train, and he could imagine its laughter if it had been switched on, cackling maniacally as though driven mad by its incarceration. But there was no laughter. The whole place remained eerily silent. He remembered that there might be rabbits in here too, or even rats, and steeled his nerves for the sound of sudden, scurrying movement.

Next to the fortune teller was a row of old-fashioned 'one-armed bandits', where you had to physically pull a lever on the side of the machine after inserting your coins. Then you would watch the dials spin, hoping for three of a kind. Given that fruit machines had a fixed pay-out rate, he never understood why people bothered 'playing' them; there was no skill involved, no peril, no story. Only blind luck that the game might be ready to cough up on that particular turn. He hurried past them, heading for the final row of machines.

Then he noticed something snagged on the arm of the last bandit. He stared at it. He walked back to the fortune teller, imagining himself as Daisy, examining the creepy clown.

He imagined someone following her into the arcade, through the door, creeping cautiously over the broken glass so as not to alert her. Someone who wanted her not to snoop around the amusement park anymore. Or perhaps simply a sadistic predator who saw an opportunity to pounce.

A struggle, right here, witnessed only by the dead eyes of the clown. Maybe screams, maybe a hand clamped over her mouth. Daisy's fortune rewritten.

Her harness snagging on the bandit as she was dragged away. Something torn loose, not noticed by her abductor, left hanging from its strap, here for Sigurdsson to find.

Daisy's video camera.

Twenty-two (The island)

Sigurdsson radioed Mitchell, and together they finished searching the amusement arcade, finding nothing else. Then they spoke with Mason and hurried back to the station.

While they had been at the murder site, Mason had already managed to find Daisy's full name and address. Daisy Higgins had uploaded dozens of urbex videos to the internet, just as she'd told Sigurdsson. From her YouTube account, Mason had found a Facebook profile, and tracked down her next of kin, a sister living in Wigan. Laura Higgins would travel down to make the formal identification the following day; what a truly awful experience that would be.

They owed it to Daisy and her family to catch her killer. Hopefully her final recording would help them. A few days earlier, Daisy would have doubtless intended to add this footage to her YouTube channel; instead, it was in a police video room, about to be viewed by three anxious investigators huddled around a small screen.

The camera's memory was full, because the footage concluded with hours of the same shot: the damaged doorway leading into the amusement arcade. The camera must have remained switched on when it had been wrenched from Daisy's harness, and had continued filming the last thing it had pointed at, until its battery ran out. Viewed in rapid reverse as they skipped backwards, the sky outside was visible, gradually changing from dark to pale blue.

The date on the footage was Thursday's. Sigurdsson's fears were confirmed; whatever had happened to Daisy had taken place the day after he had met her. He felt his hands curling into angry fists as he watched the image brighten.

Then suddenly the picture changed.

"Whoa, whoa, stop… Play it from here," Mason barked. Mitchell, struggling to operate the tiny device in his sizeable hands, finally obliged.

Daisy was crossing the road towards the arcade, just as Sigurdsson had done. It was daytime. She didn't talk on her videos, preferring to let the maudlin atmosphere of the decaying buildings speak for itself, so she simply moved slowly along and allowed the lens to linger on anything she thought would make for an interesting image. The green bunny rabbit sign outside. One of the grabber machines, full of sad-looking Eeyore dolls. A crushed-out cigarette next to a fruit machine. Sigurdsson smiled sadly when, like him, she paused at the *Point Blank* cabinet.

Soon she reached the creepy clown machine, and sure enough she stopped to capture a shot of the ghastly fortune teller. Abruptly the image snapped to the left, as the camera was dragged past the fruit machines. Sigurdsson and the others listened intently, but other than a brief scrabbling sound, there was nothing; Daisy had not even had time to scream. Her attacker had crept up from behind as she stood there, unsuspecting. Vulnerable.

The picture swayed from side to side where the camera had been snagged, eventually settling into the final shot of the doorway they had already seen.

They all craned forwards.

A large, bald, pale man was dragging an unconscious Daisy away, towards the door. He wore dark, loose-fitting clothes, and his back was turned so his face couldn't be seen. Because he was holding Daisy's limp form at his side, one arm beneath her armpits, it was easy to see that his other hand was pressing a cloth of some sort against her mouth. Ponderously, unhurriedly, he made his way to the doorway and ducked out of view, dragging Daisy behind him. His head turned slightly as he exited, but his features were immediately obscured by the shutter next to the door. They didn't get a single decent glimpse of his face.

After that, the image was still. Mitchell fast-forwarded the tape, but nothing else happened, other than the fall of night, until the tape ran out.

Silence hung like a miasma.

Then Mason spoke.

"Okay. We have video footage of the killer," she said, sounding pleased. "And there can't be that many people on the island matching his description. We could interview the ferry operators perhaps, see if anyone fitting the bill has left Salvation in the last two days. What do you think, Chris?"

A large, bald, pale man

Sigurdsson didn't say anything. Because his idea was insane.

Spitt used chloroform to incapacitate his victims.

The man had been dead for eighteen years. Yet here he was, captured on camera two days earlier, incapacitating a strong woman with ease, dragging her off to mutilate and murder her.

Continuing where he left off

"Chris?"

He looked at her and opened his mouth. Then his phone rang.

It was Erina Brennan.

"I'm sorry, I'd better take this," he mumbled as he hurried out of the video room.

When he answered, Erina's voice sounded wretched and lost. "Chris? I thought you were going to call today."

"I'm sorry. We've had... some developments, here." He knew he should say nothing at this stage. But the next of kin had been informed, and the media would doubtless get hold of it soon, one way or the other. He could imagine the headlines.

Infamous Serial Killer Back From The Dead

"What developments? Have you found David?" She sounded almost frantic.

"No, not yet Erina. I… listen, I can't tell you the details yet, but I'm working with DI Mason on a new lead. I'm not giving up on your husband. I'm going to keep working this case." He thought about Daisy, hauled out of that arcade like a farm animal selected for slaughter. Where had she awoken, when the chloroform had worn off? Tied up in a dark room somewhere? In a basement, just like the one at 58 Smalley Lane?

Alone, terrified… then tortured.

"And I'm going to do it for free. Forget about my fee."

Erina was quiet for a while. When she spoke, her voice was even meeker than before. "Thank you, Chris. You are kind. I know you're doing your best. I just wish I knew what was going on."

"I'll keep you informed, I promise. I'm sorry again that I haven't called sooner."

Dead men don't come back

"That's okay. I'm just sitting here, getting myself worked up. I can't stand the thought that he's out there somewhere, suffering."

But others can carry on their work

"Er, Erina, I'd… I've got to go, okay?" he stammered, and hung up without even waiting for a reply. He burst back into the video room excitedly.

"It's a copycat killer," he blurted breathlessly.

Mason and Mitchell blinked at him.

"The video… the rag over her mouth…" he continued. "*It's a Leonard Spitt copycat.*"

"Look, Chris. I know Lithgow is your case. I understand why you're trying to link the two. But all we have is footage of a bald man abducting Higgins. It's a bit of a stretch to say that makes it a Spitt copycat, don't you think?"

"Daisy was blonde. It matches Spitt's MO."

"Her throat wasn't cut. And besides, Spitt always worked at night. Higgins was abducted during the day."

"Maybe she disturbed him. Maybe he was hiding out nearby. Or maybe…"

She found the entrance to the labyrinth

He bit back the words. Mason thought he was trying too hard to link everything together. Maybe she was right. He needed something more tangible than the jumbled theories of a missing man.

"Either way, he can't have taken her far," he continued. "She was abducted in the amusement park, and that's where she was found, two days later."

Mason's face was tight with scepticism. "Chris, I'll need to get ready to brief my new guys. You know I can't bring you with us on the search, right?"

"I know. I'm going to head back to the house. We've only got a couple more days before Hardacre empties the place, and I'm still convinced I'll find more clues in Lithgow's work."

She didn't argue with him this time.

Twenty-three (The house)

Mitchell drove Sigurdsson back to the house. When he arrived, the first thing Sigurdsson did was wolf down one of the sandwiches he had bought earlier in the week, realising he hadn't eaten anything since he had awoken in the basement. He called Priya and left her a message saying that he would need a few more days on Salvation. He kept it vague, even though he knew she would call to interrogate him as soon as she picked it up. He ended the message by telling her which pet shop to get the fish food from if she was running out.

Then he sat for a while at the table, staring in despair at the pages stacked around him, the reams of paper adorning the walls. They seemed to tower over him, crowding in like buildings sagging in an earthquake. He needed to be away from them while he gathered his thoughts. He rose and walked upstairs, shutting himself in the bedroom Lithgow had been using, the only space other than the basement that the writer hadn't covered with his stream of consciousness. Sigurdsson sat down on a corner of the bed, which was still covered in the bedding Lithgow had been using, hastily made. He put his head in his hands, clawing at his eyes. They burned with exhaustion.

He could just leave. Tell Erina Brennan he couldn't help her, that it was in the police's hands now. Charge her no fee. Go back to his detective agency in London. Leave Salvation, and Mason, and Spitt, and Lithgow, and Octopus Girl and Anax and Doctor Mephisto and the rest of the crazy cast of characters behind once and for all.

But how could he live with himself if he did that?

We never rest

He had made a promise.

On a whim, he looked inside the chest of drawers next to the bed. The first two drawers were full of boxer shorts and socks. The third was virtually empty, other than a few odds and ends that perhaps represented the germination of a 'man drawer': a collection of batteries, a TV remote, a roll of duct tape, a marker pen.

A photograph of Brennan, in a frame. The glass was shattered.

She was smiling broadly, as if Lithgow had made her laugh and then quickly snapped the moment. A lovely picture. Once treasured, perhaps. Sigurdsson imagined Lithgow packing his belongings, preparing to move out of their family home, a tangle of emotion and bitterness and sorrow. Maybe he had thought about dashing the photograph on the floor, shattering the frame in a momentary, cathartic outburst. But instead he had packed it, carefully wrapping it within the folds of his clothes, placing it in his suitcase. Unpacking it, putting it on top of the chest of drawers, next to the bed. Every night he could lie there and stare at the face of his wife and reflect on what had happened, and remember her, and grieve for his lost love.

Then one day, in a fit of loneliness, he had smashed it after all. Just like the photograph of Spitt, he hadn't been able to bear her eyes on him.

Lithgow. A tortured soul. Sigurdsson realised he didn't have a feel for the man at all. He hadn't even found a single person on the island that Lithgow had spoken to, aside from Armitage, if the old policeman was indeed lying. It was as if the writer had consigned himself to months of enforced isolation, of absolute devotion to his project, perhaps riding the crest of one of his condition's infamous 'manic' phases.

Or maybe languishing in the depths of depression. Feeling suicidal. Resentful. Angry.

Sigurdsson thought about the ghost train at the amusement park, the carriages going endlessly round and round and round.

He thought about Spitt, and all the disturbing literature he had been immersed in for the past week. He thought about what that might do to a fragile mind, over a prolonged period.

A fascination that had become an obsession.
An unstable man having a nervous breakdown after separating from his wife

He walked down the landing and into the opposite bedroom, the one Lithgow had converted into a 'mind map'. He imagined Lithgow clambering amongst the threads, attaching new ones here and there as each inspiration came to him, scribbling more notes and sticking them to pictures, names, places, becoming confused, forgetting, writing the same thing twice. Ever more entangled in his own web.

Lithgow's mind, like a labyrinth that he had become lost in.

I have stopped taking my medication

A man obsessed with a serial killer. Shaving his head to match.

A copycat

Sigurdsson's eyes were drawn to a particular note on the wall, visible through the tangle of coloured strands. It said, 'amusement park'. He followed a bright red string from it to another note, near his head. This one said 'possible entrances'. Further threads then connected this note to others.

Chapel
Village
Museum

Using an abandoned network of tunnels to move around the island

Sigurdsson knew he was exhausted. His mind was racing. Mason would call this wild speculation, would demand proof.

But he wouldn't find it just sitting there.

Twenty-four (The island)

The light was already fading by the time Sigurdsson set out, as though the sun was being sucked slowly down into the mist like an animal trapped in a marsh. Its light burned defiantly as it sank, red and angry, making Salvation's desolate streets seem soaked in blood.

Priya had called him during the walk, as expected. She hadn't pushed him for an explanation of his actions. She had been helpful, supportive. She said he sounded tired. He said he knew.

Mason was searching the amusement park, so Sigurdsson had decided to check the other locations. He had set out into the woods, up the hill. The gradient of the incline slowly flattened as he reached the top, and the chapel appeared like something rising from the sea. It was a modest building, more like an old house, aside from the stubby tower that protruded from its northern end. He approached the main doors, glancing at the effigy of Drogo to his left. The statue's putrid green colour, caused by the oxidisation of the bronze, reminded Sigurdsson once again of things dredged from the ocean; rotten and dead, like the blighted trees that surrounded him. Yet the foot that protruded from beneath Drogo's robe remained bright and gleaming in the dying light.

He couldn't help himself. He walked across to rub the foot, making a wish as he peered up into the ravaged face that was only partly hidden beneath Drogo's cowl. He wished to find David Lithgow, and Daisy's killer, before anyone else was hurt.

Even if they were the same person

The saint didn't give any sign that he had heard.

He turned back towards the chapel doors, which comprised two chunks of dark wood, heavy and solid. He imagined them creaking open to welcome groups of worshippers, the island's blossoming population streaming through these doors every Sunday, eager to sing and repent and do whatever else they felt was necessary to avoid an eternity of damnation.

Now the doors were secured by a chain and heavy padlock, which looked like they hadn't been removed for some time. If he wanted to gain access this way, he'd need to return with more serious equipment.

He walked slowly around the building's exterior, finding all the windows boarded up. One of the planks had broken away, and he was able to peer in through a small gap. But all he could see inside were rows of pews, gathering dust, in the dark.

At the other side of the building was a smaller door set into the base of the tower, perhaps once used by the priest, who might well have lived inside the tower itself. This door was also locked, and Sigurdsson felt no give when he tested his shoulder against it.

He turned, frustrated, and noticed a pathway behind him, leading down through unkempt grass to a small collection of headstones.

This time we had a look around the little overgrown cemetery, and I spotted Spitt's name on one of the graves.

He followed the path towards the markers, which seemed to be huddled together, like old friends gossiping. Moss and weeds had grown over them, as if the earth wasn't content with accepting the bones buried beneath but wanted to reclaim the stones themselves. There were no flowers, only a riot of untamed grass choked with weeds. A sad little site. A few rabbits hopped among the headstones, nibbling and sniffing, like a desecration.

Then he noticed one grave set apart from the others, further along the path, close to the line of the trees. He walked towards it. It was denoted only by a small headstone, which looked newer than the others he had seen. A simple stone slab, facing away from the cemetery, out into the forest. As though ashamed.

He walked around to the front of it. The grave bore Spitt's name, inscribed without an epitaph.

Beneath it was a gaping, rectangular hole. Clumps of earth were piled on either side. Sigurdsson peered down into the cavity.

There was no coffin.

No corpse.

Spitt's grave was empty.

Twenty-five (The island)

"I said it's not there. Someone has taken Spitt's body."

"How do you know?"

"I'm standing at the grave right now. It's been dug up."

"What the hell are you doing there?"

"I'm checking out places that Lithgow might have visited."

Sigurdsson's head was spinning. He had walked here believing Lithgow was impersonating Spitt. Now it seemed that Spitt himself really had risen from the dead.

"Couldn't it be vandals?"

"The body is *gone*, Carin. I doubt vandals would go that far."

Why would anyone take Spitt's bones?

"We haven't found anything at the theme park yet. I think it's going to take us all night to search this place. But I can send someone out to look tomorrow morning."

Unless… the grave had been empty to begin with.

"Chris?"

"Sorry, I'm just… trying to work out how this fits."

Could Spitt still be alive?

"Chris, what you need to do is get some sleep. I'll call you in the morning and tell you if we found anything, and we'll take a look at the graveyard together."

"Okay," he replied. "But there are a couple more places I'm going to check out tonight. Starting with the museum."

"It'll be closed."

"Then I'll head to the village instead. Don't worry about me. I'll sleep when we've solved this thing."

Never rest

"Chris, you won't be any use to anyone if you collapse from fatigue. Those places will all be there in the morning. I've got to go, okay? Promise me you'll go back to Doug's and go to bed?"

He paused, feeling a strange frustration. She was right, of course. His mind was whirling, unable to process all the new information it had received that day.

"Okay, I promise," he said eventually. "Good luck."

He hung up.

The setting sun had turned a deep crimson, like a promise of violence. He clicked on his torch and searched near the disturbed grave. He found nothing of interest; no discarded shovels, no cigarette butts, no footprints.

It was as though Spitt had clawed his way out of the earth and disappeared into the forest.

Sigurdsson squeezed the bridge of his nose, trying to dispel the wild speculation from his brain. He would take Mason's advice. Even a few hours of rest might revitalise him, help him make the breakthrough that felt tantalisingly close.

Drogo observed him as he began his descent, seeming to chuckle beneath his hood.

*

As he walked back down the hill, the moon finally reclaimed the sky. It was full and bright, its light seeming to imbue the mist with an unearthly glow. Sigurdsson felt like he was shuffling through a dream. His thoughts had abandoned him altogether, his body little more than a husk, propelled forward by some shred of habit or memory.

This vessel is spent

Although it was only a short walk, it felt like many hours had passed by the time he arrived at Smalley Lane. In a daze, he unlocked the door, and went inside. He didn't even register that he had gone to the wrong place. He headed straight upstairs, towards David Lithgow's bedroom, where the broken photograph of Erina Brennan was still propped beside the bed. He climbed under the covers, like the ghost of a missing man, and fell immediately asleep.

Twenty-six (The house)

When he awoke he was in darkness. The moon's light had been snuffed out by a bank of cloud, but he didn't know this; all he knew was that it was a blackness so absolute that he felt like a disembodied presence, hanging there, his sense of self melting into the bed covers and the room around him.

Entwined with the house

At the same time, his other senses felt strangely heightened. He could taste a rancid, bitter flavour in his mouth, as if his teeth were rotting in his head. He was aware of an odd odour, something hot and heavy, like the smell of animal.

And a sound. The unmistakable sound of breathing.

Someone was in the room with him.

He couldn't move. It was more than the paralysis of fear — he felt like he couldn't distinguish his own limbs and extremities from the bed, couldn't find his mouth to open it into a scream. It was as if he was about to undergo an operation and had been injected with the most vile, sadistic anaesthetic imaginable; a drug that would keep him immobile but totally awake, hyper-sensitive to the pain that was coming. In the blackness, his mind clung to that image, and conjured up a thousand more: Doctor Harrison, approaching slowly with his scalpel, eager to cut out Sigurdsson's organs. Mason, her face twisted into a scowl of disappointment and contempt, advancing towards him with a pillow to press over his face, to erase the mistake of inviting him here. Leonard Spitt, his naked body caked in mud from the grave he had escaped, his massive murderous hands ready to crush Sigurdsson's trachea.

A creak as the intruder took a step towards him. Slowly, carefully, methodically.

He felt as if he were lying in Spitt's open grave. The giant was standing over him, preparing to tip a spadeful of earth down into the pit. He could almost feel the cold, dry soil smacking into his face. His eyes stared upwards into the black nothingness, as useless as those of a blind man. But still he could see Spitt's vacuous, haunting face. Except, as the first clod of dirt landed, he realised that it wasn't Spitt's face at all. It was his own. He was being buried by his doppelgänger.

Another creak.

The scream burst out of him then, as if his terror was too big for his body to contain. He screamed as though the last five years had been a fallacy, as though all the fear and anxiety he had overcome had in fact only been stored away, allowed to ferment, to grow and mutate into something even more toxic.

He screamed as though the sheer force and volume of his horror could drive the demon from his bedside.

He screamed so loudly that he couldn't be sure if he heard his door being thrown open and the footsteps disappearing down the stairs.

When he finally stopped screaming, his breath coming in ragged gasps as he fumbled for the bedside lamp, he couldn't be sure if he had heard anything at all.

The light came on with a click. Freezing sweat soaked his clothes and his bed, Lithgow's bed. The door was closed. The house was still and silent. He glanced at his watch. It was only 22:46.

Had it been nothing more than a nightmare?

I'm in your head now, Chris… just like I was in David Lithgow's

Sigurdsson stood, shakily. Gripping his torch like a club, he opened the door and stepped out onto the landing, switching on the light.

There was nothing there but the pages of David Lithgow's deranged book.

Somehow Sigurdsson felt even more exhausted than when he'd first clambered into bed. It was a strange sensation, as though his body had begun the process of dying. No amount of sleep or rest would be able to reverse it. He swallowed heavily, feeling desperate for a drink, like a sip of water was suddenly the only thing that mattered.

He dragged himself downstairs in a series of small movements, placing one foot in front of the other, transferring his weight, staring at the steps beneath his feet as if they might suddenly disappear and cast him into an abyss.

There was no one downstairs. No intruder. No undead serial killer. Only the photograph of Spitt on the kitchen door. He pushed it open without daring to meet the monster's eyes.

Fear makes people do strange things

Was this how Lithgow had been driven mad? This place, this hellish pressure cooker, slowly squeezing his brain until it burst? He turned on the tap and let the water run for a while, but the sound of it splashing on the metal sounded somehow off, like the wrong sound had been dubbed over the top. Clutching the kitchen work surface to steady himself, he managed to pour a glass, and gulped it down. The taste was somehow wrong too. Metallic, like he was drinking blood.

Am I still dreaming?

He poured another glass, but before he could drink it, his phone rang in his pocket.

He took out the phone, staring at it for several seconds as though he'd forgotten what it was. He drank the water, and then answered the call, words emerging from him without conscious thought, like a computer running a programme.

"This is Sigurdsson."

"Come to the village," said a muffled voice. It was a woman's, and he thought he maybe recognised it, but couldn't think clearly enough to figure out who it was. She continued, the voice's familiarity taunting him. "There will be a reunion. Tonight, at midnight. I don't want it to happen. But I can't say no."

"Who… is this?" he managed to articulate.

"Please come alone. This has all gone much too far. Maybe you can stop it. But…"

And she hung up. His memory of the call began to fade immediately, like the afterimage of lights behind his eyelids. He had to concentrate very hard, gripping the worktop until his knuckles turned white.

A reunion
Midnight
The village

He looked at the caller's number, which of course had been withheld.

He looked at his watch, which showed 22:57.

He needed more sleep. But there was no time.

Twenty-seven (The island)

As Sigurdsson headed deeper into the woods, the knotted canopy of trees blocked out the moon's pale light, and he had to use his torch to navigate. The branches seemed to grope at him, the soft touch of their leaves somehow unpleasant, like lepers pleading for alms. For a moment he was relieved when he emerged into the clearing; but then he saw the ruins, alien forms in the darkness, like monsters waiting to pounce.

A killer could hide on this island for a long time

He picked his way amongst the shapes, flicking the torch this way and that, illuminating scorched fragments of buildings, heaps of rubble. He saw a wooden sign with writing on it, explaining the site's significance to tourists. It talked about the bombing and the casualties. A small pink rabbit in the top corner of the sign wore a sad face. It didn't mention anything about gas testing, or government cover-ups, or Operation Dark Harvest.

Or beds, or sleep, or how to combat exhaustion

He passed through an empty doorway into the shell of one of the buildings, scanning left and right. The remains of a fireplace were visible, and the bottom few steps of a collapsed staircase. He thought about people sitting in their living room, or perhaps sharing an evening meal at the table, when fiery death had rained down from above.

What was he hoping to find here? A glowing neon sign above one of the buildings saying REUNION INSIDE?

In the middle of the village was a cobbled square, a small open space where the townsfolk had perhaps traded food and crafts. He walked slowly across the blackened stones towards the old well at its centre. To prevent accidents, it had been covered over with a stone slab. He hoisted himself up to sit on it, legs dangling, feeling like a child on a park bench. Feeling useless, while Mason searched the murder site. Feeling tired, so tired, tired enough to just lie down here on the stone and sleep…

Then he saw the light of torches, moving through the trees.

He quickly switched off his own light and hopped down to the ground, crabbing sideways towards the remains of a wall that stood at chest height. The lights were accompanied by voices, which started to reach him as he strained to hear above the susurrus of the evening breeze.

The voices weren't talking. They were chanting. And they were getting louder. Approaching from the north, the opposite end from which he had entered the clearing. He edged forwards, the ruined structures providing ideal cover. He could make out four separate torch beams, flickering amongst the vegetation that encircled the village. They seemed to be heading towards him. He hunkered down as they emerged from the trees.

When they did, he saw that their torch beams weren't flicking left and right, searching, like his had been. Instead they were pointed straight ahead, proceeding in single file, and as a result, the first three members of the group were lit by those behind them. He saw that all of them were wearing hooded, black robes.

Not a search party. A procession.

He watched, baffled, as the cloaked figures headed slowly towards the covered well, where he had been sitting only moments earlier. They continued their mantra, the hypnotic rhythm sounding otherworldly in the darkness, and oddly muffled, as if they were speaking through face masks.

The figures took up positions around the well, each of them stooping to place their torches on the ground beside them, pointing upwards. It gave the scene an unearthly, up-lit appearance, and

Sigurdsson was reminded of his encounter with Daisy Higgins, the day before she was abducted.

The strange, indistinct incantation continued. He crept closer, returning to his original position against the low wall, as he tried to make out their words, their faces.

One of the figures had produced a cloth pouch and was emptying something onto the heavy stone that rested on top of the well. The other three raised their hands, gesturing upwards as if they were invoking a deity. Their chant increased in volume. Suddenly a gout of flame erupted across the top of the well, like the handiwork of a teppanyaki chef. The fire blazed for a moment before it settled down, burning with a weird, greenish hue. Sigurdsson worried for a moment that the sudden illumination would enable them to see him, but he wasn't close enough to be easily visible, and the four figures seemed engrossed in their bizarre ritual. On the other hand, the unexpected blaze meant that for the first time, he could see their faces clearly.

Beneath their hoods, all four of them were wearing gas masks.

Their curious psalm continued to grow louder, more intense, although he still couldn't discern the words. The three that had 'summoned' the fire (he suspected that the first had simply held a lighter to whatever flammable substance had been tipped onto the stone) kept their hands aloft, while the fourth member reached into their robe once again, this time producing the dead body of a rabbit. With one hand, it was held above the dancing flames, which seemed to reach hungrily for the creature's flesh as the chanting rose to a crescendo.

Then, in unison, the others produced three long knives from inside their own cloaks. The blades glinted in the firelight as they each slashed at the carcass, one after the other. The flames sizzled and leapt as the rabbit's blood dripped onto them. The animal's body was passed around the circle, each one taking a turn at holding it, shaking it, encouraging every last drop of gore to fall into the emerald conflagration.

Whether there was a predetermined number of times that the poor creature's body had to change hands, or whether they were waiting until it had been completely drained, was unclear. Either way, after a while the corpse seemed to have served its purpose, and it too was tossed into the flames. The group gave a final, climactic cry, all four pairs of arms raised as if in celebration as the fire roared briefly. Then, one by one, their voices dropped, and their hands fell.

But Sigurdsson had already spotted something. Their hands were all bare, their pale skin visible in the fire's greenish glow. Aside from establishing that they all belonged to white people, he could discern little from seven of them. But, unlike the others, the eighth didn't have four fingers and a thumb. Instead it was a single, tapering appendage, almost like an octopus's tentacle.

Lucy Chen. That's whose voice he had heard on the phone. She had been the one that had summoned him here.

But why?

A reunion, she had called it.

The four of them quickly cleared away the remnants of their ceremony, sweeping the ashes and the rabbit's carcass into a bag. If they were speaking to each other, then it was quietly, and Sigurdsson could not make out a word. He held his breath and stayed very still, not wanting to alert them in the unexpected silence. They bent to pick up their torches, and again he was gripped by a sudden fear, that they would turn towards him, catching him in the glare of their flashlights. But instead they walked back the way they had come, to the north.

If he called Mason now he would risk losing them. And besides, Chen had been very insistent that he should come alone.

He waited until they had crossed the line of the trees and then followed, treading carefully but swiftly in the darkness.

Twenty-eight (The island)

It was impossible to be silent in the forest. Branches were rustled by Sigurdsson's passing, and twigs cracked underfoot. But thanks to their torchlight, he was able to keep the group in sight while maintaining a safe distance, and they showed no sign of having detected his pursuit. They simply continued to march purposefully through the trees, like sinister druids on a strange pilgrimage.

The tangled branches above his head prevented him from seeing the lighthouse looming above until Chen and her group had almost reached it, emerging from the forest into an open area around the base of the old building. Sigurdsson hung back, crouching amongst the drooping leaves of a willow tree, and watched as they approached it. The lighthouse was another of Salvation's landmarks that he had never visited before, and although it was illuminated only by torch beams and the moon's pale light, he could see that it was another crumbling, abandoned relic. The white paint had cracked and peeled away from its exterior, and the railing encircling its main beacon was completely rusted. He wondered what business the group could possibly have there.

They ascended a small staircase to the main door, which had been covered over with a sheet of metal. He wondered if they were going to produce yet more equipment from their cloaks, perhaps a crowbar to prise it open. But instead, they simply stopped, and knelt close to the door, as if in prayer. Was this another ritual? He edged forwards, towards the last line of trees.

A rabbit burst out of a pile of leaves a few feet to his right.

He froze. Four masked faces turned immediately towards him.

There was only a single tree between him and them. He was protected by the darkness, but only if they didn't shine a torch in his direction.

Meanwhile, the rabbit tore into the open like a thing possessed, running straight towards the group. At the last second, it seemed to sense their malign presence, and veered off to the left, skirting the outside of the lighthouse and disappearing into a nearby burrow.

The masked faces followed it.

Sigurdsson didn't move. He didn't breathe.

Three long knives, glinting in the moonlight

In unison, they turned back towards the door.

He exhaled, relieved, and hunkered down.

One of the group rose and approached the door, bending towards a small panel next to it. They lifted their gas mask, and Sigurdsson craned his neck to try to see their face; but whoever it was had their back to him, and he couldn't catch a glimpse. They spoke something into the panel, slowly and in what sounded like a man's voice, but he was too far away to make out what was said.

The metal sheet across the door slid open, and the four of them hurried inside. Seconds later, it moved back into place with a mechanical whirr.

He waited. He didn't want to be caught in no man's land, out in the open, between the woods and the lighthouse. But he needed to know how they had gotten inside. What he had thought was a simple metal screen to prevent vandals from accessing the derelict building seemed to be a fully functioning security door – but why on earth would one of those be installed on an abandoned lighthouse?

If they were inside to conduct another bizarre sacrament, or indeed for any meaningful purpose, it would take time. Therefore, the longer he waited before investigating, the more likely they were to re-emerge and apprehend him.

He took a deep breath and walked calmly through the long grass towards the door. No one came out. There was no sound from inside. All he could hear was the wind, moving ominously through the trees behind him. Adrenaline pumped in his veins, blasting the tiredness from his system. But he knew the exhaustion was still there, lurking inside him like a dormant illness.

The lighthouse towered above him, maybe forty feet high. It must have once been of vital importance to visiting sailors. Now, it was just another of the island's artefacts; another corpse for the seagulls to pick at. One of the tourist guideposts was planted in the ground close by, the bunny logo in the corner smiling this time as its speech bubble explained that the lighthouse was constructed in 1807 to service the northern bay, which had once been a busy port and fishing harbour. The helpful rabbit also informed visitors that the structure was currently closed to the public.

Yet four masked strangers – more accurately, three masked strangers and one enigmatic barmaid – had just walked inside.

He placed his hand against the door. The metal was smooth and solid, not merely a flimsy shutter as he had thought. He wouldn't be able to force his way inside. He looked at the panel to the left of the door, into which one of the group had spoken. It was some sort of intercom, but with no buttons. Could it be a voice recognition unit? Or perhaps there was a guard, listening at the other end, granting entry to those who knew the correct password. A guard who could be watching him, even as he stood there. His head darted from side to side, looking for a camera.

He saw nothing. Only the baffling doorway, a puzzle that he couldn't solve. There was still no sound from behind it. He couldn't risk standing here for much longer.

Perhaps he could wait them out, hidden amongst the trees.

He retreated towards the woods, dissolving back into the darkness.

Twenty-nine (The lighthouse)

His eyes stung. He badly needed to sleep. His eyelids felt like they were hung with heavy weights, and even that thought set his brain wandering down a strange path, imagining bodies suspended from the ceiling, with hooks pushed through their flesh; corpses hung from walls inside a tiny house; his own body, sliced open like a flayed rabbit, like Daisy Higgins.

Like the Minotaur beneath the blade of Theseus.

He jerked his head upright, blinking. His watch said 02:35, which meant he had been crouching here for over two hours. The group hadn't reappeared. He had turned off his phone, not wanting to risk any noise or light, but now he thought about checking it, in case he had a message from Mason, in case she had found something.

But he couldn't leave this post. Mason would either still be out searching the theme park, or else she would be in bed. Either way, he shouldn't disturb her. If nothing had happened by dawn he would call her, and they could find a way into the lighthouse together. Maybe the masked strangers were sleeping in there.

Sleep

He could imagine its embrace, could feel the allure of its temporary amnesia. The pile of leaves at his side looked like the most luxurious bed he had ever seen. He thought about Mason, in her house with the red front door, and wondered what her face looked like while she slept. Or perhaps she was lying awake, missing her daughter, who was doubtless staying with a babysitter once again. He thought about Holly, growing up without a father because he had taken his own life. A bipolar sufferer, like Lithgow. A complex disorder, once known as 'manic depression'; surprisingly common, with 1 in 100 people suffering from it at some point in their lives.

Lithgow, pouring out his troubled soul onto paper.
Piles of pages.
Piles of leaves.
Piles of dirt.
An empty grave.
The bald man in the video.

Spitt would have had to duck down, because he was almost seven feet tall. But this man hadn't. He had passed beneath the doorframe as easily as Sigurdsson had.

Lithgow, who had lived alone, like Sigurdsson.
Lithgow, who was six feet two.
Possible entrances.
Chapel.
Village.
Museum.

Lighthouse?

An idea exploded into his mind, blasting through the leaden ooze of fatigue. He stepped forward, striding quickly through the grass, as he had done earlier. He approached the sliding door once again and bent to the intercom panel.

"Dark Harvest," he said into it.
There was silence.
Then the door slid open, revealing only darkness beyond.
No one came out. There was no sound except the soft breeze moving through the leaves behind him, like ghosts.

He took a deep breath. He clicked on his torch and pointed it into the gloom.

Inside, a spiral metal staircase led upwards towards the lighthouse beacon. The steps were rusted, and the walls were grimy. The floor was covered in debris and dark stains.

And footprints, in the dust. They surrounded an old-fashioned trapdoor in the centre of the floor. It was made of wood, and had a thick iron ring. He walked towards it.

The door hissed shut behind him.

Thirty (The island)

Mason awoke at six to her alarm's familiar ditty, and clicked it off irritably. She never used the 'snooze' function, as she'd rather have half an hour of additional good quality sleep, instead of thirty minutes or more of fragmented tossing and turning. The flip side of that coin was that when the alarm sounded, she had to get out of bed *immediately*; a single, painful jolt into the new day. But it was a routine she'd become accustomed to.

She hauled herself up and planted her feet next to the bed, her toes grasping at the carpet as though for support. Her first thought, as always, was of Holly, before she remembered that her daughter was staying at her friend's house again; like she so often had to, because she had a dead father, and a terrible mother.

Be kinder to yourself, Carin

Her next thought was of Chris, and she glanced at her phone to see if he had returned her calls. She'd left him a frustrated voicemail late the previous night to say the search had proved fruitless, and that they were calling it quits. Nothing back from him yet. She hoped he was sleeping. The case was taking a strange toll on him. She wondered about his motivation, why he cared so much about Brennan and Lithgow. She worried that somehow, he was doing it for *her*, and then she berated herself for being so egotistical.

She stood up and made her way to the bathroom, the icy coolness of the tiles on her soles helping to wake her. She cleaned her teeth, frowning into the mirror at the wrinkles appearing around her eyes. Then she showered, feeling the grime of the previous night's efforts clinging resolutely to her skin. The feeling of scavenging through a murderer's territory had made her feel contaminated, like she had been wandering inside a building infested with rats.

But the vermin she was looking for had eluded her. The killer hadn't left a trace. There were no footprints, no clues aside from the camera Chris had already found. The only loose end was some sort of maintenance access point they'd found close to the Ferris wheel, sealed off by a metal door that they'd been unable to prise open. They were planning to return with a cutting torch, but she wasn't optimistic it would yield anything helpful; the door had presumably rusted shut long ago.

She thought again about Sigurdsson, her friend. He had used that word, when he had been here two nights earlier. She supposed that was the best way to describe their relationship. They certainly weren't colleagues, or partners. And they had never even kissed. So 'friend' was really the only option.

Except it didn't seem to describe the way she felt about him. She knew that she had recommended him to Erina Brennan because she had wanted him to come here. It had come to her in a moment, the words tumbling out of her mouth before she'd even had time to think them. And now here he was, back on Salvation. Being sucked into David Lithgow's chaotic world of killers and cultists and labyrinths and conspiracy theories.

Her fault.

However, she felt about Chris, whatever he was to her, she knew she was worried about him. When she had finished showering, she phoned him. Once again, the call went straight to voicemail.

*

Before she headed to the station, she drove to collect Holly from her friend Olivia's house. Like everything on Salvation, it wasn't far away. Olivia's parents lived in the northwest corner of the island, in one of the bigger houses close to the bay. Whenever she visited them, Mason felt worried that her daughter would compare their own modest home and would begin to resent her for not being able to provide such a nice big bedroom, such expensive toys, such a huge TV.

But, as usual, Holly beamed broadly when she saw her mother, and all of Mason's paranoia and self-doubt instantly melted away, like dirt wiped from her skin. She knelt and held her arms open in the doorway, and Holly ran towards her to give her a huge hug.

"Honestly, it's no trouble, we can take both of them to school too," said Shawn, Olivia's dad. His wife Debbie was hidden away upstairs, working on something to do with her graphic design job.

"No, Daddy! I want to go in the police car!" Olivia shouted, staring demandingly up at her father.

"Shhh, Olivia," Shawn scolded mildly, ignoring her. He addressed Mason again. "Seriously though, I heard about… what happened, in the paper. How dreadful. You must be very busy."

He was right. But Mason wouldn't miss seeing her daughter for anything. If she couldn't be there to put her to bed, she could at least be there in the morning, to drop her off at school.

"It's fine," she replied. "Thank you for having her again."

"No trouble at all. She's been as good as gold."

It was a well-used turn of phrase, but as Mason looked into Holly's cherubic features, and saw the energy and playfulness radiating from them, it seemed somehow appropriate. Corn-coloured hair, which had grown lighter than her mother's in the last few years, fell around Holly's freckled face, and her smile was wide and honest and sweet. Mason's daughter truly seemed to gleam, like gold, in the wan morning light.

"Right, come on then, girls, otherwise we'll be late, and I'll have to put the siren on," Mason said as she rose to her feet.

"Can we?" cried Olivia.

"Not unless we're chasing baddies," chided Holly matter-of-factly, and Shawn laughed. But Mason could barely manufacture a smile as she thought again about Daisy Higgins's last video.

Mason had seen a baddie. A man who had mutilated a woman and left her to bleed to death in the dark.

However long she could shield Holly from the reality of her work, of the world, would not be long enough.

She hugged her daughter again. "Say goodbye to your dad," she said to Olivia, who grudgingly returned her father's embrace. Then the two girls ran down the driveway, holding hands.

"Bye, officers!" Shawn called as they clambered into the squad car. Mason waved once before she slid behind the wheel, trying to concentrate on enjoying this precious time with Holly, instead of thinking about what she'd like to do to Higgins's killer.

Thirty-one (The island)

When Mason arrived at the station she phoned Sigurdsson again. Still nothing. She left a message asking him to call, then headed to the main operations room, where Mitchell was already waiting for her. The other PCs that had joined them for the search the previous night were staying at the Grand Hotel, and she'd told them not to report back until eleven, to make sure they got enough sleep after their late finish.

She and Mitchell would just have to suck it up.

Usually Clive would be there too, ready to head home after his late shift, but she'd asked him if he could join the investigation team for the next few days, so he would be there at eleven as well. This meant they'd have no one in the station overnight, so she would be on call if any emergencies came through. At least there was no one in the cells.

A skeleton crew. A quiet island outpost, not set up to handle a murder investigation.

At least she felt more comfortable asking for support these days, unlike when DCI Wells had been her commanding officer. Wells had been a chauvinist, constantly plotting against her, until he had been sacked five years earlier for his misdemeanours. Her new boss, DCI Rampling, was excellent, if a little humourless. Mason called her to report on the evening's lack of progress, and Rampling suggested that she focus on Higgins's connections on the island, on anyone the dead woman knew here or had been seen with. Her sister's visit to formally identify the body would be an opportunity to gently interview her. Perhaps she could find out who Higgins's friends were, who she had spoken to in the lead-up to her death. The phone company could help with records of outgoing calls before Higgins's phone had been switched off.

People she had been seen with

Mason hadn't yet told Rampling about Sigurdsson, or his involvement in the case. She knew she would have to, and that Rampling would want her to cut him out of the investigation team altogether, to treat him as a suspect.

Chris… where are you?

"What's the plan for today, boss?" asked Mitchell in his usual gruff monotone, approaching her desk. She looked up at him, seeing a man she trusted. A man she was proud to have on her team.

"I want to go and look for Sigurdsson," she said, matter-of-factly. "I'll be back here to brief the team at eleven. Then we've got Higgins's sister arriving at midday. While I'm out, can you make sure we haven't missed any of the ferry operators? And get an image extracted from the video, something we can share with the public. Someone must have seen this bald fucker… and we need to warn people that he's dangerous."

Mitchell nodded, and went to work, like he always did. Initiative wasn't her sergeant's strong point. But he was obedient, diligent, hardworking. Reliable.

"And we should get the diving crew back to sweep the bay one last time, for Lithgow," she called after him. Then she headed downstairs, detouring to take a quick look at the reception area, to make sure there was a sign explaining that it would be unmanned that day, and what number to call. A skeleton crew.

She opened the doorway and saw the little desk, the computer, the chair in the corner. She'd spent many days covering that desk herself, alternating the task with Mitchell, and with Giggs before he had been transferred.

She also saw a woman outside, banging on the glass front entrance. A woman with dark glasses, and dark hair held up in a red headscarf.

Erina Brennan.

Mason closed her eyes and sighed, then crossed the reception area to open the door.

Be nice, Carin. The poor woman is worried about her missing husband. She won't accept he's dead until you find the body. That's just the way it is. You'd feel the same.

"Hello, Ms Brennan."

"I've been knocking for over five minutes," came the angry reply.

"I apologise. We have a busy workload today, so we're unable to man the front desk. I was passing and saw you through the window. Please, come inside."

Brennan followed her into the station, looking pale and agitated.

"I'm sorry. I'm glad you're busy. Have you... made any progress with David?"

"We'll let you know as soon as we find anything, I promise. I'm sorry we haven't got more to tell you right now. We're working closely with Detective Sigurdsson."

And you turning up here is going to put him under more pressure, she almost added.

Brennan was visibly distressed, as though she wanted to push past Mason into the police station and satisfy herself that they weren't all lounging around and drinking cocktails in the back room.

"I couldn't sit there at home any longer. It feels like nothing is happening!"

Mason closed her eyes, trying to summon up reserves of patience. She knew this wasn't her strong suit; she was short-tempered, passionate, fierce. 'Fiery', people often said; although that was mainly because of her ginger fucking hair.

"I assure you, Ms Brennan, we're doing everything we can to find David."

"I've been calling Detective Sigurdsson this morning, and there's no answer. Do you know where he is?"

He's probably at your husband's madhouse, sleeping, thought Mason. She had to find a way to stop Brennan from going there.

"Detective Sigurdsson is at your husband's house, working on some leads," she replied. "But he's specifically asked me to ensure he's undisturbed until the afternoon."

Brennan stared back at her, a maelstrom of emotion seeming to hide behind the dark lenses of her glasses.

"I'll be at the Restful Inn," she snapped eventually, and stormed out of the station onto the promenade, where the mist waited to swallow her up.

Mason hurried towards the car park at the station's rear, clambered back into her vehicle and drove as fast as she could through the winding streets towards Smalley Lane. She was worried she would see Brennan on her way there, but the poor woman seemed to have obeyed her instructions for now.

When she arrived, the street was silent and still. The fog was even thicker here, the house seeming to lurk within it, like a skulking prowler. She parked outside and approached the front door; knocked and waited. There was no sound from within. She dialled Sigurdsson and got his voicemail once again.

She took out her key and opened the front door. Inside, her note was still pinned to the living room door, which made her smile briefly. She pushed it open.

And gasped.

Her note was the only page that had been left behind. The others were gone. The walls, the table, the teetering piles that had littered the living room: they had all vanished.

She ran up the stairs, bewildered. Everything had disappeared. The kitchen, the bedrooms; all were empty, every shred of Lithgow's work seeming to have simply blinked out of existence.

Calm down, Carin. There had to be an explanation for this. Perhaps Hardacre had reneged on their deal and started the clean-up of the house earlier than they had agreed. But why would he leave Sigurdsson's blow-up bed lying there? And where was Chris?

She called him. Voicemail. She called Hardacre's house on the island. No answer.

Sinking into the sofa, she tried desperately to think. She imagined Chris doing the same thing, then tearing off to follow a hunch, some careering train of thought that had lurched suddenly away. Maybe he'd taken the pages with him. But why? And how would he transport so many documents without a car?

The Marine View. Of course; he was probably just asleep at Doug's place, like she had suggested.

It took her only a few minutes to reach the bed and breakfast, where she found Doug busy hoovering.

But he told her he hadn't seen Chris since Friday morning, two days earlier. She thanked him, asking him to ensure the detective called her immediately if he arrived.

Climbing back into her car, she reclined in the driver's seat, exhaling deeply as she tried to figure out what to do next.

The museum. Chris had talked about going to the museum, and the village.

Places Lithgow might have visited

She drove north, the road meandering through the forest until an empty car park appeared on her left. She would stop here and check out the village first, before she followed the road onwards towards the former convalescent home.

The morning breeze was cold and pitiless as she hurried along the path through the trees. The rabbits seemed to be hiding from its icy chill, and she saw very few of them as she walked. She had visited the ruins recently with Holly, the same day they had been to the museum together. Holly had thought the village was boring, but Mason was fascinated by the weird shapes of the wrecked buildings, like the fossilised bones of something huge and prehistoric. Now they loomed before her once again, an otherworldly landscape swathed in mist.

She looked around, not sure what she was expecting to find, circling slowly towards the central square. The fog made her feel like she was drifting through a dream, the buildings materialising suddenly as she approached them, as if from thin air. She reached the cobbled plaza and saw the well at its centre, imagining Sigurdsson following a similar route, perhaps feeling the same frustration that there was nothing here.

A large stone rested on top of the well. As she approached it, she noticed an odd, ashy residue coating its surface, as if someone had lit a fire there. Kids, probably; they often came here to mess about amongst the ruins, drink alcopops, smoke cigarettes. She wondered if Sigurdsson had also found the sooty deposit, reached out to touch it, rubbed it between his fingers.

She called out his name. Then she called it again, and a third time.

Silence. Other than a few rabbits, the only life here was Mason herself, small and alone in the dead heart of the abandoned settlement. Even the birds seemed to have departed, as though they had finished picking the village clean.

It was like Chris Sigurdsson had evaporated into the clammy air.

Thirty-two (The island)

Mason navigated a different route through the ruins on her way back, but still found no trace of him. Climbing back into the car, she headed for the museum. The road snaked through the trees as it ascended a gradual incline and then, as she crested the hill, the forest suddenly thinned out, the ground falling away into a large and picturesque expanse of grassland. Soon the road narrowed into a gravel path, and a sign advised her to leave the vehicle in the car park to the left and continue on foot. She did so, noticing only one other car in the small allotment. Cronin's, perhaps. Meaning there were no other morning visitors, unless they had walked here.

The path led her down the hill and towards the grounds of the former convalescent home. The building had been carefully restored after its destruction during the war, and was a sprawling neo-gothic edifice, its dark brickwork seeming to defy the sunlight as though it was hewn from a giant block of obsidian. Gargoyles crouched menacingly amongst the intricate masonry of the parapets, gables and chimneys. The central tower looked like a colossal spike driven upwards from beneath the earth, an ominous sliver of rock crowned with a clock face that gazed down at her like a great unblinking eye, observing her approach with fascination. The place looked more like an insane asylum than somewhere for wounded soldiers to heal.

A rusted metal fence marked the boundary of its grounds, its spiked gates propped open. She passed between the gateposts, gravel crunching beneath her feet as she approached the large main doors of the building itself; these also stood open, with one of the little tourist signposts nearby, incongruent with the imposing surroundings.

'The Salvation Military Convalescent Hospital was opened in 1916 to support the First World War effort,' said a grinning pink rabbit. 'Over a hundred thousand soldiers stayed here to recover from their injuries during the hospital's active service, which spanned both World Wars, until its destruction in 1940. The faithful restoration of the building was financed by Thomas Hardacre, and this museum was opened to the public in 1973.'

Mason crossed the threshold, entering the cavernous main hallway. The ceiling stretched away to the roof above her, an oddly extravagant chandelier suspended above a grand staircase that split into two as it curved upwards to the second floor. A sign at the bottom of the steps reminded her to head upstairs for the exhibits, apologizing for the lack of disabled access. The large doors to either side of her were closed off, leading to rooms she had never been in. Maybe that was where Bill kept his waxwork creations when they were not in use. She shivered as she imagined storerooms full of deformed mermen and misshapen monsters.

"Bill?" she called, but once again found herself answered only by stifling silence. She headed towards the stairs, passing the 'honesty box' that asked for a minimum donation of £5 for entry. Inhaling the museum's dusty, mildewed odour, she hoped that Cronin was being allowed to spend the money on maintenance, rather than it going straight into Hardacre's pocket. She wondered how Cronin managed to keep on top of things here, with what appeared to be no staff whatsoever. Maybe he didn't. Maybe it was crumbling around him, like everything else on this godforsaken shithole of an island. She thought again about Holly, about whether she owed it to her daughter to take her to the mainland, to a better school, to somewhere that felt like it had a future. Then she thought of Olivia, and Holly's other friends. She thought of Mitchell and the police station. She thought of her house with the red front door.

The years ticked by, and still here she was. As though Salvation didn't want her to leave.

She dropped a ten-pound note into the box and ascended the stairs.

There was still no sign of Cronin as she reached the second floor, and a notice pointing toward the alien exhibit, which made her smile. This had been Holly's favourite part. The sign directed Mason through a pair of double doors, after which the walls were covered with silver façades to make them appear metallic, as if she was now wandering inside a spaceship. Along one wall was a timeline of UFO activity on the island, while the other was inset with little 'observation windows' that showcased pieces of meteorite, framed photographs of alleged sightings, and fragments of implants apparently recovered from abductees.

It was all utter nonsense of course, but she could see Cronin's mischievous hand at work, and felt saddened that there weren't more visitors.

She continued along the corridor and passed through another door that claimed to require 'Area 51 security clearance'. The room beyond was decorated to look like the control room of a spacecraft, a little like the bridge in *Star Trek*, except the crew were neither human nor Vulcan; they were short, humanoid aliens with huge eyes, like something out of *The X-Files*. Half a dozen of the creatures occupied the chamber, manning flight controls, operating computer systems, peering into video screens. Each one was incredibly lifelike; the grey flesh stretched across their gaunt frames looked like it would be soft and yielding, and the dark ellipses of their eyes seemed to glisten wetly with malign intelligence.

She lingered for a while, marvelling at Cronin's handiwork. She almost expected one of the creatures to turn to her, aiming a ray gun and demanding to know how she had hijacked their ship. On the opposite side of the room the wall had been painted to look like outer space, viewed through a front window (she wondered whether they were called 'windscreens' – she had never been a big sci-fi fan). Mason found herself mesmerised by the swirl of stars, as if she really was speeding through the cosmos. She turned to leave.

Then she screamed.

Thirty-three (Nowhere)

Sigurdsson stretched out a hand, because he needed to lean against the wall for balance. And to reassure himself that something down here was real, and solid.

Because everything else was madness.

The wall was covered in bones. Skulls, femurs, pelvises, ribs, teeth… they were embedded in the cement, arranged into strange, cyclical patterns. But at least they were real, the alternating roughness and smoothness beneath his fingers, the cold and unforgiving stone, then bone, then stone, then bone.

What else was real? The gas he had breathed… that was real. Idiot. The reason they had worn masks was because these tunnels were poisoned. He hadn't been thinking clearly, had followed them down here like a brazen fool. Now his mind was in disarray, and at every turn it conjured images of horror; of monsters, of rabid dogs, of mutilated women, of people he loved staring out at him from the walls. Screaming. Beseeching.

Stay down here with us, Chris, murmured his father. He ignored the invitation, turning another corner, deeper into the maze, deeper into the island's black heart. But it didn't help. He knew that his father would appear again soon, the bones and teeth arranging themselves into a twisted approximation of the old man's features. Or maybe it would be his mother, her face ravaged by illness, her eye sockets gaping and empty.

The strange thing was, he wasn't afraid. Instead, he felt *angry*. More than anything, he just wanted these spectres to leave him alone.

To let him concentrate on the hunt

The staircase had led him to a long corridor whose walls were smooth, featureless concrete. There had been strip lights set into the ceiling above him, their bulbs long since burnt out. The air had smelt sweet and sharp, as though lemons had been squeezed over everything.

After a few hundred yards, he had begun to pass metal doors with electronic keypads set into the walls next to them. Other corridors branched off from this main central tunnel, and he had seen more of these doors at regular intervals along them. The entrances to testing areas, perhaps. Or cells.

He was in the abandoned laboratory, exactly like Ian Skelton had described.

When Sigurdsson had reached the first junction and turned right, he had been confident that he could remember the way back. But a strange, lightheaded feeling had begun to cloud his thoughts, blurring his memory like smeared ink. He became more and more convinced that he needed to press on, taking turns at random, speeding up as his pursuit gathered impetus. He had a very clear idea that the group were just a few metres ahead of him, that he was faster than them, faster and stronger. That he could catch them and *slit their throats* find out what was going on here. He realised he had forgotten the way back to the lighthouse, but he didn't care. Eventually the path led him right up to one of the metal security doors, this one larger than the others, and standing open. They must have come this way, he felt sure of it.

He could smell their fear

Beyond the door, the tunnels became more uneven, at times resembling a natural cave network. As if he had walked backwards through time. He had a dull sensation of being a foolish explorer, of disturbing something ancient and evil. But as the citrus stench became stronger and stronger, he became more and more bold, more determined. Onwards he went *stalking his prey* as the catacomb became steadily more complex, its winding tunnels coiling and looping back on themselves. He was hopelessly lost. His brain seemed to be battling with itself.

> *This place is contaminated, Chris*
> *Nerve toxins*
> *Chemical weapons*
> *Who knows what the gas is doing to your lungs, your brain*
> *That's why they wore the masks*
> *That's why this island is full of rabbits*

Don't listen, Chris. Just keep going
Soon you'll find those fuckers and then you can beat the truth out of them
Break their fingers one
by
one
That torch you're holding clubbing their
skulls into powder

That's when the bones had started to appear, adorning the walls as though marking the entrance to a monster's lair. That had been lifetimes ago.

Now all he knew was the maze.

Every labyrinth needs a Minotaur

A sound to his right, like cautious footsteps in the darkness. The Minotaur was slow, but patient. He veered left, stumbling as his head swam, almost falling over.

You must be so tired… come and rest down here, Chris.

He reeled backwards, cowering from the face of his brother, Marcus, who had died horribly when he was only a child. Marcus, trapped down here, in whatever circle of Hell Sigurdsson had blundered into.

Stupid idiot child. It was all his fault
Their family had fallen apart all because he couldn't stay out of the
road.

No.
    Not Hell.
    Not Marcus.
    Only tunnels, and some sort of airborne hallucinogen.
    Sigurdsson struck a hand against his own head, trying to force
himself to think clearly.

Another footstep, closer

Hunting, in the darkness.

But who was hunting who?

He hurried along the passageway, taking turn after turn, trying
to shake off his pursuer. His torch beam danced across the walls,
revealing fleeting horrors that grinned at him as he raced past.
The vapour seemed to be thinning as he ran, and he was able to
breathe more easily… but that didn't stop the hellish visions from
tormenting him.

You failed your parents and now you're failing Erina Brennan
Everyone you love ends up dead
Chris… who will look after Holly now?

It was the sight of Mason's face, imprisoned amongst that sea of
faces, that was finally too much for him. He stopped to stare at her
contorted features, reaching out to touch her, to tell her that he
was sorry. But Mason just laughed at him, her husky voice rising
to a shrieking cackle as terrible as the wail of a banshee, and as
she laughed her face melted away, and he was pawing at a leering
skull, another anonymous victim.

Who had done this, had buried these people down here, in these forgotten caves?

So many missing persons cases still unsolved

Spitt… how many more women did you boil to bones and drag down here into your dark kingdom?

A soft hissing sound, only metres away from him. He imagined snakes squirming and writhing around a hideous face, one glimpse of which would turn him to stone.

First the Minotaur… and now the Gorgon

What menagerie of horrors dwelt down here?

None, Chris
It's all in your head.

He staggered away from the sound, concentrating on the walls, trying to count the dead. It was impossible. Their remains were mixed together, their identities lost in Spitt's profane mural. Nothing remained of the people that had once inhabited this jumble of bones.

Anonymity
Desecration

A page, stuck to the wall.

He snatched it, stared at the typeface, recognised it instantly. A single sentence.

This is your fault

He moved along the passage, aware that the hissing sound was still following him, like a huge serpent was slithering in his wake. He found another page, and another.

Why couldn't you help me?

All I wanted was happiness. A wife. Children.

You left me to rot.

Loser

Weirdo

Freak

You didn't believe in me.

You told me I was a monster. Remember when you said that?

You're a MONSTER, David.

I'll show you what monsters can do

The trail led Sigurdsson onwards. Ten metres, twenty, thirty. So much vitriol poured out onto the paper. A man's pain and rage, hammered out on the keys of an old typewriter, brought down to decorate this dreadful sepulchre by a lonely man, a delusional man, a depressed man, a man who had lost touch with what was real and what was imagined.

David Lithgow.

His body was slumped against the wall, a few feet after the pages stopped. His legs were splayed out into the corridor, his hands clasped in his lap as if he was simply taking a moment's rest during a long walk. There was a plastic bag over his head, a suicide device that Sigurdsson had seen used before: known as an 'exit bag', you pulled it tight using a drawstring while pumping gas inside. The small canister by Lithgow's side had probably contained helium, or nitrogen – breathing it would bring about rapid unconsciousness, while the absence of carbon dioxide alleviated the sense of suffocation and panic.

Sigurdsson removed the bag. Beneath it, Lithgow's features were gaunt and sallow, and his head was shaved. *A large, pale, bald man.* But his expression was peaceful, and he still resembled the man in Erina's photograph. In his lap was one last note, a final page he had chosen to cling to as he died.

> *I'm sorry, Erina*
> *David loved you so much*
> *But now he's dead*
> *Now there is only*
> *The Minotaur*

Sigurdsson stared into the dead man's open eyes, and saw utter emptiness there, a terrible and absolute oblivion.

This vessel is spent

Sigurdsson heard the serpent-like sound again then, this time right behind him, but as he tried to turn, his brain seemed to yaw to one side within his skull, and he lurched sideways into the wall. He looked up groggily, into a face hidden behind a gas mask. His assailant was holding one of the long knives, raised upwards, the pommel of the weapon aimed at his head. Breath hissed as it was drawn through the mask's air filters.

Like a snake

The blow came down ferociously onto the top of his skull.

Bones, bodies, fears, horrors, rabbits and warrens and tunnels and trees, light and darkness, life and death and gravestones and earth and rot and snakes and skulls and bones

All of it faded, like forgotten things buried long ago.

Thirty-four (The island)

"I'm sorry, I'm so sorry, I didn't mean to sneak up on you!" Cronin fussed around her, apologising repeatedly.

"It's alright, Bill." Mason waved him away, blushing. "I'm just bloody embarrassed; I don't 'do' screaming. Where did you appear from?"

"I was wandering past and saw you from the other end of the corridor, so thought I'd come and say hello. I really am sorry for startling you. Can I get you a glass of water perhaps?" He looked completely different without his 'Doctor Mephisto' ensemble – nothing more than an old, bald man wearing comfortable jeans and a threadbare jumper. He seemed to walk with more a stoop when he wasn't performing, although he was still taller than her.

"No, honestly, it's fine. And I'm sure you don't have time to offer drinks to everyone who visits."

"Yes, well, it's a quiet day, as you can see." He looked downcast for a moment, and then seemed to brighten up. "So, do you like my extra-terrestrials?"

"They're awesome. Remember I told you I brought Holly here recently? She loved this bit."

He smiled modestly. "Be sure to tell her I'm working on something else that will *really* blow her away." He wiggled his eyebrows, and Mason laughed. "Anyway, how can I help you, Detective Inspector? I presume you aren't here just to visit the crew?" He gestured at the assembled aliens.

She shook her head, hesitating for a moment before deciding to reveal her current plight. "To tell you the truth, I'm here searching for Detective Sigurdsson. He hasn't contacted me since last night, and this morning I can't find him anywhere."

Cronin frowned. "I'm sure I don't need to ask if you've phoned him. Where is he staying?"

Mason hesitated again. "He's... been staying at the Leonard Spitt house."

"I see. And you've already been there, of course. Perhaps he's just out and about, somewhere with bad phone signal?"

"He *was* out and about last night, as it happens. He mentioned that he was planning to come here, to the museum, but I told him it would be closed. I don't think he's thinking clearly... he's been working very late, not getting enough sleep. I don't suppose you were here late last night yourself, or if there was any sign of him when you arrived this morning?"

"As it happens I was here *all* night, working on my new exhibit. The one benefit of being a lonely old bachelor is that no one minds when you don't come home." His smile was laced with a twinge of regret. "But I'm afraid I saw neither hide nor hair of anyone."

It was Mason's turn to frown. "Okay. Thanks, Bill. I'll be sure to bring Holly back soon. When does the new exhibit open? Can I ask what it is?"

"You can ask, but then I'd have to kill you..." He grinned devilishly, transforming into Doctor Mephisto again, just for a moment. "It should be opening in a few weeks' time."

She laughed again. "I'll be sure to tell Holly about it – she'll be excited. Thanks anyway, and sorry to have disturbed you. I dropped you a tenner in the honesty box by the way; don't spend it all at once."

"That was very generous of you. I would bow, but I think I put my back out doing the old Mephisto routine midweek."

"You need to take care of yourself, Bill. I have no idea how old you are, but I imagine it's too old to be doing that sort of thing."

"How dare you!" he scolded playfully. "And besides, it depends who you're asking – Bill Cronin, or my alter ego."

"Why, how old is Doctor Mephisto?"

He winked at her. "Oh, he's been around forever... in one form or another." He seemed to find this remark very funny and carried on chuckling as he turned to walk away. She followed him along the corridor, laughing politely, even though she didn't quite get the joke.

The old rascal bade her farewell at the top of the stairs and shuffled off towards another wing of his domain. She watched him go, then descended the stairs, unsure what to do next.

She walked back to the car, called Sigurdsson, got his voicemail again. Then she drove towards the centre of the island, where Chris had told her he'd found Spitt's grave, desecrated; if it was even possible to desecrate something that was utterly unholy in the first place. Once again, she had to leave the car parked on the road and complete the journey on foot.

At the top of the hill, the first thing she saw was – of course – that bloody statue. She ignored the horrible, gangrenous thing, and circled the chapel once, confirming that the building was locked up and undisturbed. Then she followed the path down towards the tiny cemetery. It hadn't been used as the island's main burial place for a couple of centuries, and was overgrown and neglected, but the decision to bury Spitt here still seemed odd to her; personally, she'd have rather seen him cremated and tossed in a landfill site somewhere, but she hadn't been in charge at the time. His grave was set apart from the others, further along the path, close to the trees. She could see the signs of disturbance even before she reached it, two heaps of earth piled on either side of the headstone. As she approached, she saw that Chris was right; the actual grave itself had been dug up, and its contents were missing.

She shook her head in bafflement, making a mental note to arrange for the hole to be filled in while they added the missing cadaver to their growing list of unsolved mysteries. She wondered how long Spitt's body had been missing; and more importantly, where it was now, and for what purpose it had been exhumed.

Trudging back to the car, she sank into the driver's seat, called Sigurdsson, got voicemail.

She exhaled; a long, exhausted, frustrated sigh, feeling like her strength was seeping out of her along with the breath.

She felt distraught and useless as she drove a few more aimless circuits of the streets.

Helpless… just like Erina Brennan

She stopped the car. She imagined Sigurdsson's body stretched out on Greg Harrison's gurney, battered and broken by similar injuries to those that had killed Daisy Higgins. The pathologist's skilled fingers peeled back his rib cage as she looked on, nauseous, her friend's dead eyes fixed on her. It was a sudden, powerful image, and she felt briefly appalled, and horrified, and panicked, all at once. She needed to find him. But she couldn't think of anywhere else to look.

Then she thought of somewhere.

Thirty-five (The house)

Mason drove immediately back to Smalley Lane, climbed out of the car, and approached the house once again.

A desperate, last ditch idea.

"Chris? Ms Brennan?" she shouted as she unlocked the front door and stepped inside, conscious that Lithgow's wife might be there. But the house remained silent, seeming to gleefully swallow up Mason's words. She glanced once again at the note she had stuck to the living room door. But this time she didn't head that way; instead, she reached for the handle of the door to the basement. As her hand closed on the metal, an irrational fear squirmed in her guts, like a twisted knife. She swallowed hard, and yanked the door open.

Even though she knew the staircase would be dark, the sight of the steps descending into blackness paralysed her.

"Chris?" she shouted, hearing nothing in response. Even the echo seemed to have been silenced somehow, absorbed by the gloom beneath her. Behind her, the house felt empty. But somehow she couldn't shake the feeling that something was waiting for her at the bottom of the staircase.

She reached forward to turn on the light. The switch clicked uselessly – the bulb must have gone. She swallowed again, her mouth feeling suddenly dry. There was nothing else for it; she took out her torch, aiming the beam down into the dark pit. Then she took out her baton and descended, listening. Other than the creak of her footsteps, the silence remained absolute. She felt like each footfall was taking her closer to some nameless horror.

She reached the foot of the staircase, shining the torch around, her heart battering against her ribs.

The basement was empty.

She breathed another deep sigh and felt angry with herself for allowing an element of relief to enter it.

This was it. Her last throw of the dice. For all she knew, Sigurdsson was now another missing person, another body they would soon recover from a patch of wasteland.

Then something caught her eye: a tiny fragment of white, at the bottom of the wall opposite. Frowning, she walked towards it. There was a small white triangle on the ground, where a featureless patch of the wall met the floor.

The corner of a piece of paper.

She tugged on it, and an entire page slid out easily, as though there was somehow a gap beneath the wall. The single word DESCENT was written on the crumpled sheet. On the other side was one of Lithgow's rambling, indecipherable narratives.

She tossed it to one side and felt along the join between the wall and the floor. If there was an opening, it was barely wider than the piece of paper had been. But why on earth…

She moved her hands upwards, searching the wall with her fingers, wishing she had better illumination than the torch she was holding between her teeth. But it was just a solid breezeblock wall, exactly like the rest of – wait. There was a vertical crack, running upwards in a straight line. She rose from her knees as she traced it to above head height, then followed it as it turned a right angle to run sideways for a few feet, then back down, all the way to the floor. The outline of a perfect rectangle.

Or a hidden doorway.

She almost tripped as she sprinted up the stairs and back out to the car.

"You're late for the meeting," Mitchell said when he answered her call.

"Forget the meeting. I want all five of you here, right now. I'm at the Spitt house. Bring the breaching tool."

*

The false wall collapsed easily, showering the five of them with a cloud of dust. They stared down a tunnel into a blackness that seemed even more absolute than the darkness of the basement itself.

Mason felt her mouth hanging open but couldn't seem to work out how to close it.

A secret passage.

She thrust her torch further into the opening. The strange portal led into a short, narrow corridor, constructed from the same simple breezeblocks as the rest of the basement wall. At the end of the passage was a T-junction. Mason led the way, gripping her baton as she stepped into the space. When she reached the junction, she whirled to her right, the torch revealing another passageway that stretched away indefinitely in a sharp downward incline, with various other openings branching off from it.

An underground labyrinth, just like Chris had suspected. Right under their noses. Was *this* where he'd gone?

She spun and shone her torch the other way, expecting to see another network of intersecting tunnels. Instead, the beam revealed a single wooden door, only a few feet away from her. It was standing open.

"What can you see, boss?" called Clive from behind her. But she was staring, dumbstruck once again. Beyond the door was a large room, with a few steps leading down into it, granting it more height than the cramped corridor.

On the opposite side of the room, a corpse had been attached to the wall.

It had long ago rotted away to nothing more than bones, but these had been affixed together so that it retained its humanoid structure, like something that belonged in the ghost train. The skeleton's arms were spread out as though it had been crucified, but it was hanging the wrong way up, arranged in a blatantly satanic symbol with its feet in the air and its head close to the floor. Candles were arranged at the base of this disturbing figure, making the room seem like some sort of macabre shrine.

Mason remembered Alice Goldsmith, the teenager that Spitt had flayed and positioned in the same fashion in the living room upstairs. But these remains were much too large for a teenager. They stretched virtually from floor to ceiling, despite the increased height of the chamber. Almost seven feet.

A giant

Why would someone do this with the killer's remains? Or were these merely a fake; some sort of perverse, elaborate hoax?

She walked towards the room, flicking the torch to the right, illuminating a featureless wall. To the left was a rickety wooden desk and chair. There were more candles on the desk, as if it was perhaps being used as a workstation. Maybe Lithgow had found this place and had been using it as a sort of study.

Or perhaps he had built the shrine himself.

"Fuck me," she heard one of the other policemen murmur as he stepped down into the room behind her. Then he coughed, and so did Mitchell. Mason felt it too, a sudden tickle in the back of her throat, as if the air down here was full of dust.

Or as if they were breathing something noxious.

Entombed beneath his house of horrors, Leonard Spitt grinned back at them, in the darkness.

Thirty-six (Somewhere)

Awake. An explosion of agony in his head.

"What are we going to do?"

A hard surface beneath him. His head hanging down, unsupported, as though off the end of a too-short bed.

"We'll have to kill him."

His eyes blinking open, staring upwards into darkness.

"We're here to kill the copycat, not a policeman."

"He's not a policeman."

Torch beams flickering, illuminating a high and featureless ceiling, studded with strip lights.

"It doesn't matter. The copycat already did the job himself."

"How did he even get down here?"

Straps at his wrists and ankles, holding him down.

"Maybe he found one of the other entrances."

"He's breathed the gas."

Muffled voices, breaths that hissed like monstrous things.

"I think it's dissipated, over the years. He doesn't seem affected by it."

"Can't we just… leave him tied up here?"

Unable to move. Rising panic in his guts.

"What, and let him starve to death? That's worse than killing him."

"We have to get rid of *everything*. That was the purpose of our reunion."

A male voice. Stern, commanding… and familiar, despite the distortion.

"I don't want to do this."

A female voice, also one he recognised.

"We have no choice. He knows about us."

"He doesn't know who we are. He hasn't seen our faces."

Figures peering down at him, briefly visible in the torchlight. Gas masks making them seem alien and frightening.

"Shut up, Mina. Do you want them to find out about what we did?"

"It's already too late! Have you *seen* what he did down here? Their bones are *in the walls*… oh God, what have we done?"

Two women and two men, arguing about his fate.

"Bram should decide. He is the leader now."

A pause. Breath passing through air filters, a harsh sibilant sound. Slow. Calm. Unhurried.

No one coming to save him.

"We kill him. We feast, like the old days. Then we burn this place, and all the evidence, and both of them."

"No! We can't–"

"It's what Vlad would have done, Mina."

"Oh, stop with the stupid names, Donald! All that rubbish about eternal life, the blood of the earth… the True Whisper didn't save him, or Leonard, did it? Look at us… look where we are, what we've become!"

The crack of a blow, a startled cry. Soft sobbing.

"Your words dishonour our Church, child. Vlad was our enlightened leader. And even Nosferatu, misguided and foolish though he was, was our brother. Their names must be honoured."

Donald… Leonard… the names spun in his mind like letters dancing on a page. He tried to tie them to faces, voices, memories.

"L… Lucy…" he coughed.

"Shit, he's awake!" yelled the other woman.

Someone grabbed his hair roughly and struck him across the face with a savage backhand blow.

"You will be *still* and *silent*," his captor commanded. Sigurdsson blinked upwards into the masked face, made ghastly by the eerie torchlight. He twisted his head to pull free of his tormentor's grip, to try to see more of his surroundings. They were in a long room of some sort, the utilitarian décor resembling the corridors he had first found beneath the lighthouse. He was strapped to one of many metal gurneys that stretched away from him in both directions, perhaps half a dozen on either side. They were all empty, except for the table directly to his right. There, Lithgow's corpse had been placed, and piles of paper heaped around and all over him, like some sort of bizarre monument. The paper was covered in writing, typing, drawings, notes, scribbles. It looked familiar.

They had taken it from the house.

He turned his head again, and saw the cultists, all still wearing their robes and gas masks. Lucy Chen was cowering on the floor, knocked off her feet by the force of the blow she had been struck. But his gaze was drawn instead to a small metal trolley near his head, the type you might expect to see in a hospital or a morgue, laden with medical apparatus. This one held only one instrument: a large, ornate, cruelly serrated knife, with symbols carved into its hilt, like something ceremonial. Something potent with ancient dark magic.

Wrenching his head further to the side, he saw that on the ground beneath him was a large, wooden bowl.

What on earth were they planning to do to him?

The male cultist who had been identified as the leader stepped away from him, approaching Lithgow's body. Sigurdsson stared as the man produced a cloth bag from inside his cloak and emptied its contents all over the dead man and his work.

The powder. They meant to burn David Lithgow, and all of his records, to ash. And then Sigurdsson himself would be fed to the green fire.

But before that…

The knife
The bucket
The vampiric pseudonyms

… they intended to feast. He heaved against his bonds, bucking and twisting, howling with effort as he tried to wrench a limb free. But one of the other cultists sprang at him, tugging his head downwards by his hair, holding the strange knife at his throat. The wickedly sharp blade gleamed and sparkled in the torchlight, seeming to glow with power. All he could do was stare as the leader produced a lighter and moved it towards Lithgow's funeral pyre. The knife was cold and absolute against his flesh. An ending.

He closed his eyes.

Then there was an unearthly howl, and *something* tore into the chamber.

Chaos erupted all around him. Light danced on the walls as torches were aimed towards the noise. The cultists shouted, in confusion at first; then, as gouts of blood began to spray, the shouts turned to screams. A monstrous shape careered amongst the robed figures, growling, rending, roaring with delight.

The knife at his throat clattered to the floor nearby. Sigurdsson hauled again on his bonds, his muscles bunching, veins feeling like they were about to burst with the strain. Suddenly his right arm tore itself free, and he felt a surge of euphoric relief. He reached down and beside him, feeling for the knife, glancing around him as he did so at the unfolding insanity.

One of the cult members had fallen close to him, clawing at their mask, yanking it off to reveal an unfamiliar woman's face contorted in the throes of death. Blood spurted from a hole in her neck. All he could do was stare as she bled out, twitching like an insect.

What was going on?

He hacked desperately at his bonds, sawing his left arm free and rising to a sitting position so he could tackle the straps at his ankles. That was when he saw Lucy Chen, illuminated by a fallen torch. She was screaming, flailing uselessly beneath the hunched shape of a monster.

Anax.

Hardacre's enormous hound was poised over her, her gas mask dangling from his teeth like a dead animal. His fur was matted with dark gore, blood dripping from fangs that looked like rows of saw blades. The beast tossed the mask aside, then bent towards Chen, sniffing at her. She turned her strikingly beautiful face briefly towards Sigurdsson, almond-shaped eyes wide with absolute, paralysing terror.

Then Anax sank his teeth into her cheek, and blood splattered the dog's face, and she screamed.

Sigurdsson attacked his bonds once again, the leather straps parting beneath the knife's razor-sharp edge. He had no idea how or why the creature was down here. But if he didn't get free soon, Chen would die, and he would be powerless to defend himself against Hardacre's monster. Chen's shrieks continued as Anax bit again and again at her face, working himself into a frenzy of excitement and bloodlust.

As the straps binding Sigurdsson's ankles finally came loose, a shot rang out, the muzzle flash flickering briefly at one end of the long room. The dog yelped and leapt away from his prey.

Another shot. Sigurdsson hurled himself off the table before he was caught by a stray bullet, feeling the wind knocked out of him as he crashed to the floor. The dog, shot twice, staggered in a wide semi-circle, whining, only a few feet away from him.

Two more shots resounded deafeningly in the strange laboratory. Illuminated briefly in the muzzle flare, Sigurdsson saw another of the cultists lying prone on the ground in a spreading pool of crimson. Anax reared up and howled in pain and confusion, then stumbled forwards onto his face.

Sigurdsson scooted backwards away from the beast, pressing himself against the wall as he tried to remain in the shadows. The roar of the gun faded, and for a while the only sound was Chen's cries of pain, echoing horribly.

Then footsteps, as the man with gun stepped forwards into view, illuminated in the beam of a fallen torch. His height and sturdy build marked him out as the cult's leader; the last one standing. He approached the motionless animal, prodding hi tentatively with one foot, the gun trained on his improbably huge carcass. He seemed not to notice Sigurdsson, who gripped the knife, eyeing the open doorway in one corner of the room… but Sigurdsson didn't want to risk revealing himself to an adversary who still had bullets left in his gun.

Chen's screams had faded to whimpers as she crawled away from the creature that had nearly mauled her to death. The cult leader ignored her too. Sigurdsson could hear the man's breathing through the mask's filters, still strangely calm and measured, as he aimed his pistol at the dog's huge head.

Sigurdsson didn't move. He stared at the deranged tableau that had unfolded before him, a scene of carnage and strewn bodies: Lithgow, Chen, the two other cultists, Hardacre's blood-crazed hound. Sigurdsson stared at the wooden bowl that had been placed beneath his own head, at the ceremonial carvings on its sides.

One deep cut across the throat and his blood would flow into it, like a slaughtered animal

There was a sound. A booming, fearsome, horrifying roar of pure rage, like a noise disgorged from hell itself; the sound of the most intense pain and fury and suffering imaginable, combined into one single deafening cry and unleashed into that strange underground place. It came from Anax, who lurched suddenly to his feet, and leapt at his tormentor like a vengeful demon.

The tall, strong-looking man was tossed to the ground as if he weighed nothing, pinned beneath a frame more like that of a horse than a dog. The titanic canine's powerful chest heaved, his fur matted with a mixture of his own and his victims' blood.

The monster had been shot *four times*. How could he still be alive?

The fallen man stretched his arms upwards in desperation as the beast snapped at his face, trying to clamp Anax's bottom jaw closed. But the dog was too strong for him. Slowly his powerful neck muscles forced his massive head downwards, his mouth yawing open, spilling blood into the man's masked face. With another monstrous howl, Anax bit savagely at the mask, wrenching it free with ease, and then sank a sickening bite into the flesh around the man's eye. The cultist shrieked in pain, writhing and bucking beneath the dog's immense bulk.

But some part of him, perhaps nothing more than instinct, was determined to survive. Sigurdsson watched, transfixed, as he managed to bring the gun up, and fire two more rounds point blank into Anax's enormous skull. The dog reared upwards onto his hind legs, a clump of flesh hanging from his teeth, and roared once again; the sound seemed to shake the very walls themselves.

Then the noise fell suddenly to a whimper, and Anax slumped sideways, scrabbling at the air.

The man staggered to his feet, gasping and clutching at his eye socket, and emptied two more rounds into the dog's massive body.

The sound of the gunshots faded. The beast was still. Lucy Chen had fallen silent, hidden somewhere in the shadows. The only sound was the cultist's breathing, heavy and laboured, his wide shoulders rising and falling as he stood over the body of the seemingly indestructible hound.

But Anax didn't rise again.

Slowly, with his back to Sigurdsson, the cult leader walked towards David Lithgow's body. The cultist bent to retrieve his lighter from the floor nearby. Then he touched it to the scattered powder, and Lithgow and his bizarre book burst into emerald flame.

For the first time, Sigurdsson saw the cult leader clearly as he turned, unmasked and illuminated in ghastly green. He was a big and burly man, but old, the lines of his face like deeply carved incisions. His right eye was a ruined mess, blood dripping down his cheek and chin; it looked like the orb itself was gone. The nightmarish vision faced him, raising the gun.

Sigurdsson had never met the man, but he knew exactly who he was. Chen had used his real name earlier; and, somehow, everything was beginning to make an insane kind of sense.

"Stand up," barked Donald Armitage.

Armitage, who had been listed as a possible cult member.

Armitage, who had lied about speaking with Lithgow.

Armitage, who had apparently found Leonard Spitt dead in his cell, all those years earlier.

Sigurdsson rose slowly to his feet, trying to keep the knife hidden behind his back.

"You. How did you…?" Armitage began, until his words were lost in a strangled groan of pain; he tottered, clamping a hand to his ravaged face.

"You need a doctor, Donald," Sigurdsson said carefully. "And so does Lucy."

The gun came up again. The fire blazed behind Armitage, casting strange shadows, like ghosts dancing on the walls.

"And why wouldn't I just kill you? No one else knows what's happened here. I can easily disappear. Go back to my retirement."

Sigurdsson's mind raced. He needed to get the gun. If it were a police-issue ARV pistol it would be a Glock 17, carrying seventeen rounds in its magazine. Armitage had fired eight shots into the dog… which meant that he probably had plenty of ammunition left.

"It's like you said before, Donald," Sigurdsson replied, trying to sound calm. "You didn't come down here to kill innocent people. You were searching for Lithgow, and you found him." He nodded towards the flames that blazed with green fury like something unnatural.

A sudden panic gripped him. The gas… was it flammable?

"That thing… is that Ed Hardacre's dog?" Armitage rasped, seeming not to care about the rising inferno behind him.

"Yes. I have no idea why it was down here. But it means there are probably others coming, Donald. Why don't you give yourself up? We can leave together, before this whole place explodes."

Armitage stepped forwards, the emerald glow making him look like something toxic. The wreckage of his eye made Sigurdsson wince.

"It's Detective Sigurdsson, isn't it? I spoke to you on the telephone. Tell me – how did you find us? Did *she* tell you about the reunion?"

He pointed disdainfully towards the dark corner into which Lucy Chen had retreated. Despite the light from the flames, Sigurdsson couldn't see her; perhaps she had already fled the chamber altogether. Or perhaps she was already dead.

He had to believe that Anax's appearance meant that someone else was down here, and had heard the screams and the gunshots, even if it was only Edward Hardacre. Sigurdsson played for time, trying not to think about the fact that Hardacre hated his guts, and had been listed by Lithgow as a possible cult member himself.

"No… I was just investigating the village, and saw you all," he lied. "I don't understand what's going on here. Or why you lied to me on the phone." He coughed as acrid smoke began to billow out of the fire, burning his tired eyes. "If you're going to kill me anyway, why not tell me?"

Armitage smiled cruelly. "What, like the ending of a film? I tell you my big master plan, and then someone appears to save you, right at the last second? I don't think so."

He raised the pistol, squinting down the barrel.

"Then at least tell me one thing," Sigurdsson blurted, feeling his heart pounding as adrenaline churned in his arteries. The vile smell of cooking flesh clogged his nostrils. "You're all named after vampires. You're Bram Stoker… Lucy is Mina Harker… Leonard was Nosferatu… but who was Vlad?"

Armitage's one good eye twitched as his finger tightened on the trigger. Then he seemed to change his mind and shrugged. His face took on a strange, wistful expression.

"Vlad was the founder of our Church. He remade this island, and he remade each of us." He cast his eyes downwards for a moment, looking remorseful. "Vlad's earthly vessel was known as Thomas Hardacre. We followed him… together we found these tunnels, the old laboratory. And the gas, still bottled up. We breathed it and knew that the answer was to be found in blood. The secret of eternal life. So, we started with the rabbits, and by drinking some of each other's… but it wasn't enough."

"So it was *all of you* that killed those women? Not Spitt?"

Armitage's expression hardened. "You must understand; none of us *wanted* to kill them. But it was necessary. Nosferatu brought them to us, that we might feast. That was his job, his contribution to the Church. Sometimes he administered the killing blow, sometimes me, sometimes others. But we didn't expect him to be the one to… have an attack of conscience." Armitage shook his head sadly. "And now look at us. Age caught up with us, after all."

"*You* killed Spitt, didn't you, Donald? In his cell?"

Armitage snorted. "The big dumb idiot brought it upon himself. He released the gas in these tunnels, made them impossible to access, handed himself in at the police station. We… I… found the bodies in his house. I remember his smile, while he confessed. The mindless fool."

"So, you already knew… what you said to me, about the horrors you found in Spitt's house… you already knew what you would find, because you all did it, together?"

Armitage shook his head. "We weren't monsters. We just needed the blood. Vlad gave Nosferatu that house because it is directly connected to the catacombs."

Sigurdsson's eyes widened.

"Yes, that's right," Armitage chuckled maliciously. "I visited you in that house several times this week. I could have killed you while you slept."

The noises… the nightmare about someone in his room

"But back then, we never went into the house. Spitt used to bring us the women, and he used to clean up afterwards. None of us knew what he was doing in there. None of us knew that he was coming down into the tunnels alone, covering them with his… *artwork*. That lunatic destroyed our organisation. And a year after Spitt was caught, Vlad was dead."

Armitage reached up again to clutch his damaged eye, swaying woozily.

"So why do this? Why the reunion, if you'd all gotten away with your crimes, managed to pin them on Spitt?"

"Because this *pretender* wouldn't let it rest," Armitage snapped, whirling to face the bonfire that was consuming David Lithgow. "We are the last survivors of the Church. We decided it was best to eliminate him, before any more secrets were... disturbed."

Sigurdsson took a cautious step forwards, tightening his grip on the knife behind his back. "Donald... all you have to do is walk out of here with me, and everyone can know what happened. All these bodies can be put to rest. You don't have to carry this secret with you anymore. Think of all those families. It might not be what Thomas would have wanted, for his Church. But look around you." He gestured at the carnage surrounding them. "The Church is gone."

He took another step, but Armitage noticed his advance, and spun to face him again, pointing the gun. Smoke swirled between them, the flames crackling as they chewed through David Lithgow's body. "That's enough now, Detective," Armitage coughed. "You're right; it's time to leave. So, turn around, and get down on your knees."

Sigurdsson stood, motionless. He had run out of ideas. He felt his whole body tense. "You know I can't do that, Donald."

Armitage shrugged. "Suit yourself," he said, and fired.

The shot hit Sigurdsson in the hip, spinning him around. He gasped at the intensity of the pain, so sudden and concentrated, like a splinter of pure agony driven into his side. He fell to the ground, staring upwards at the ceiling, as he had been earlier when he was tied down like a calf in an abattoir. The knife clattered uselessly to the floor.

Armitage stepped into view, calmly aiming the gun at Sigurdsson's head, just as he had done to Anax. The old man's expression was tinged with regret, but determination burned in his one remaining eye, and his jaw was grimly set.

"D... Donald..." Sigurdsson gasped through the pain. "Carin... DI Mason... she always respected you. She wouldn't... want this."

Armitage opened his mouth to say something, then closed it again, and nodded sadly.

Then the ex-policeman staggered backwards, twitching and jerking as though suffering from some sort of violent seizure. He crashed into the burning table, the flames leaping gleefully onto his body as he dropped to the floor.

Sigurdsson heard shouts and cries of shock, and tried to roll onto his side, to see what was going on. But the pain in his hip was too much. For the second time in as many hours, his battle against unconsciousness proved futile, and he slipped into merciful oblivion.

The last thing he saw was Armitage's face, contorted in a terrible grimace of pain, as the green fire began to devour him.

Thirty-seven (North Devon District Hospital)

A beeping sound, regular and reassuring

The corroded figure of Saint Drogo standing over him, writing something in a clipboard

A great, shaggy dog, crouched at the end of his bed

Images, drifting through his mind. Some real, some imagined.

Nurses lifting him to change his bedding

Someone wheeling him through intersecting corridors, deeper into the maze, as strip lights passed overhead

A beautiful woman with red hair telling him he had better bloody well wake up

The remnants of the gas, perhaps, or just an exhausted brain trying to process all that had happened.

A Minotaur lying dead in the centre of its labyrinth, its head covered by a plastic bag

A doctor entering his room, speaking to him, asking him questions

"Detective... are you awake?"

Sigurdsson's mouth, dry as ash, filled with a vile taste.

"Ummm… yes?"

He tried to sit up, but the doctor stepped forward and eased him back down. She had a harried demeanour but a kindly face.

"You need more rest."

"How long…?" Something itching beneath his nose, and in his arm.

"A day. Don't touch that."

He was picking at the itches, finding tubes there, synthetic things connected to him.

"You were very lucky. You lost a lot of blood."

"What happened to… Armitage?"

"I'm sorry, Detective. I don't know the details of what happened to you. The police have been to see you already. I'm sure they'll be back with explanations. Please, try to sleep for now."

Carin… she had saved him.

He sank back into his pillow and felt the fog envelop him again.

*

The next time he awoke, the room was dark.

I could have killed you while you slept

Sigurdsson jerked upright, feeling a painful tug in his arm, and yanked the catheter out. He had a buzzer in his hand and pressed it frantically. Silence, except for the monotonous beep. A private ward. He tried to slide his legs off the side of the bed, but they didn't seem to be working.

A nurse bustled in. "Oh, dear," the short, hassled-looking woman muttered. "You need to relax, sir. Don't try to get up."

"I need to call Mason. I need to find out what happened."

"Please, just lie back. Oh, look at this mess." Blood was dripping from his arm, staining his sheets. "I'll go and get the doctor."

A different doctor entered shortly after, a man this time, who looked even more stressed than the nurse. He reattached

Sigurdsson's drip, but had no answers to his questions, except for his last one.

"What's wrong with my legs?"

"You were shot in the hip. We are hopeful you'll be able to walk again, but it will take time."

He blinked numbly.

"Can you contact DI Mason for me?" he said eventually. "I want to speak to her, right now."

"I'm sorry, sir. It's very late. I know you're disorientated, but please go back to sleep."

"What about the gas I breathed?"

The doctor consulted his clipboard. "We've been monitoring you closely, and so far you seem to have suffered no ill effects."

"What was it?"

"We don't know."

Frustrated and confused, Sigurdsson eventually lay back down, thinking that he would have no chance of resting, until sleep reclaimed him moments later.

*

The next day he awoke to be told the police were there to see him.

At first, he was confused when Mitchell entered the room. For a second, a horrible thought crossed his mind, that Mason herself had also been hurt during the violence. Or killed.

But she entered right behind her sergeant, and Sigurdsson felt that familiar, hot feeling in his gut, and a broad smile spreading across his face. When her eyes met his, her face lit up with a mixture of delight and concern.

"*Finally* you're up!" she yelled as she dashed over to him. She paused for a moment, then seemed to give in to an impulse, and hugged him tightly.

"Not 'up' exactly," he remarked when she finally released him. "But they're hopeful I'll walk again."

"That bastard," Mason snarled. "He's dead, you know. Mitchell Tasered him; we saved him from the fire, but not before his fucking old black heart gave out."

Sigurdsson glanced at the burly sergeant, who had lowered himself into a seat and was fiddling with the buttons of his uniform. "That's twice you've saved my life. I don't know what to say."

Mitchell shrugged awkwardly. "No worries," he muttered.

Sigurdsson couldn't help but chuckle at his typically stoic response, and Mason did too, and before he knew it they were both laughing uproariously. Even Mitchell managed a smile.

"So… what happened?" she said eventually. "How the bloody hell did you end up down there?"

"Nope. I'm the poorly one, remember? So, you have to go first. How did you find me?"

"You won't believe this, but there was an entrance under the house."

"Armitage told me. He said he came inside several times while I was sleeping there. I was convinced one night that I heard someone in the bedroom; I thought it was just a nightmare."

"There was a hidden door in the wall. Like something from the Famous fucking Five."

"But… why was Anax with you?"

"He wasn't. Bloody Hardacre turned up while we were at the house, to start clearing out the place. Brennan was with him, trying to stop him. Before we knew what was happening, the dog had dashed off into the tunnels."

"And it led you straight to us?"

Mason nodded. "And that's not all. As well as a way into the tunnels, under the house we found a… sort of a shrine."

"What do you mean, a shrine?"

"Spitt's body, hung on the wall, surrounded by candles. We think Lithgow put it there. God knows when he did it."

"Jesus… and Erina saw that?"

Mason shook her head. "She didn't go into the tunnels. Hardacre did, chasing after the dog, but came back out coughing and choking, saying something about a strange smell, like gas. We had to get breathing equipment before we could go in. We only have two bloody gas masks, so it ended up being Mitchell and me. Budget cuts, and all that."

"The gas… that must have been what drove the dog crazy. It happened to me, too… I felt this intense anger. Almost like *bloodlust*. Armitage was talking about them all breathing it as part of their rituals. They'd found a batch of it, still bottled in canisters, down in the laboratory."

"What else did he tell you?"

"It sounds like Hardacre Senior was trying to start up his own religion, a sort of… blood-drinking cult. Brought on by the gas, I suppose. Spitt kidnapped women for them and brought them to the island. They met in the underground laboratory, killed the women, drained their blood. They thought by drinking it they were achieving eternal life."

Mason gazed at him as she continued, her expression twisted into one of revulsion.

"Spitt was supposed to dispose of the corpses. But instead he was… using them for other things. And not just in his house… there were dozens more bodies in the catacombs. Probably all unsolved missing persons cases, from the mainland."

"We saw them. Their bones, their teeth, decorating the walls. It's like Dante's Inferno down there."

"So I guess this is a lot bigger than your team now?"

"Yup. The island's crawling with police. There's talk of a huge clean-up operation, maybe even evacuating Salvation while they get rid of the gas."

"So, the fire didn't cause an explosion?"

"Whatever it is, it doesn't seem to be flammable."

"Is Ed Hardacre involved?"

"He claims not to know anything about it. We can't pin anything on him, except for the dangerous animal. Although to be honest, Anax has kind of come out of this story as the hero."

They both fell silent.

"I suppose we'll never find out everything about the Church," she continued eventually. "They're all dead."

"Wait… what about Lucy Chen?"

"What about her?"

"She was one of them. She was the one who called me to tip me off about their 'reunion'. I think she was having second thoughts about what they were doing, what they'd done."

Mason frowned. "We only recovered four bodies: Armitage, Lithgow, Marion Weisberg and Lucas Hanley. Marion worked in the supermarket, and Lucas worked at the visitors' centre. I've known both of them for years. It's crazy."

"Chen was down there too. She was attacked by the dog before Armitage shot it. I think she got away. She could still be lost in those tunnels for all we know."

"Or she got away and left the island. Shit."

"I think she wanted to atone for her part in it… She must have been very young when the True Whisper first resurfaced."

"We'll find her," Mason said solemnly.

They were silent once again.

"So… are you okay? After breathing that stuff?" Surprisingly, the question came from Mitchell.

Sigurdsson shrugged. "The doctors seem to think so." He looked up at the sergeant, at the scar curling upwards from his neck to his chin like an unanswered question. Mitchell nodded back at him. "It's Wayne," the big man said eventually.

Sigurdsson didn't understand. "What?"

"My first name. You asked me what it was. It's Wayne."

Sigurdsson smiled.

"Nice to meet you, Wayne."

Mitchell nodded again, having seemingly exhausted his supply of words for one day.

"Anyway," Mason cut in. "Now it's definitely your turn. I want you to tell me *everything* that happened to you since we last spoke."

So he did.

Thirty-eight (London)

From: erinab82@acemail.com
To: never_rest@sis.co.uk
Date: 15th August
Subject: thank you

I'm sorry it has taken me some time to get in touch with you. It has been very difficult for me to come to terms with what has happened. But I want to thank you for everything you've done – without you I would still be searching for David, still wondering, still unable to move on with my life. Now, although it fills me with sadness, at least I know that he was truly gone. The David I loved was consumed by his illness. I don't blame him, or anyone else. I can only apologise for the hurt and pain he caused before he took his own life.

I would like to pay you for your services, double the fee we originally agreed. I only wish I could afford more. Please contact me with payment details and I will arrange for an immediate bank transfer.

Best wishes,
Erina

She had sent the email several weeks earlier, but he had not yet replied. She'd left him a few missed calls since then, and once again he found his finger hovering over her phone number. But he didn't really know what to say. Erina had lost someone very dear to her in terrible circumstances. And accepting her money wouldn't ease her suffering one iota.

He didn't call. Instead he scrolled to Priya's number, and found her still in the office, despite it being after seven pm.

They chatted for a while, Priya bringing him up to speed on the case she was working, an online identity theft.

"It'll be great to have you back, Sigs."

"I hope I won't get in the way. I'm not as mobile as I used to be."

"Don't worry. I'll just have to do all the legwork while you keep the office tidy."

"God, I bet the place is like a bombsite."

"Tidiness is subjective. My system is just *different* from yours. Anyway, how's Casper? Is he missing me?"

"He's got his hands full at the moment, actually. I've got visitors."

"Really? Who?"

"Don't sound so surprised. I have friends other than you, you know."

"Ooh, I've been promoted – I thought I was more of a lackey."

"Speaking of my visitors, I'd better go and check on them. Don't work too late, lackey."

"Yeah, yeah. Slave driver."

"Bye, Priya."

"Bye, boss."

He smiled as he hung up, then rose from the edge of his bed, leaning on his cane as he hobbled towards the door. He could hear the *Batman* DVD as he approached the living room. She had asked what detectives do, so he thought that might be a fun way to explain it. It was the classic animated version from the 90s of course, the one with Mark Hamill as the Joker; she might need a few more years before the Tim Burton movie was suitable.

He opened the door. She wasn't watching the DVD. Instead she was on the other side of the room, staring into the fish tank.

"Where's Casper?" she said, not turning, her eyes fixed intently on the glass.

"He's probably hiding. You're much bigger than him, remember. He probably thinks you're scary."

"I'm not scary!" she protested. "Can I feed him? Then maybe he'll like me."

"Of course you can."

"How many worms is he allowed?"

"Just one for now."

"Can I eat one?"

"No, you can't; they're only for fish. They're… poisonous for humans."

Holly Mason turned to him, frowning as though trying to weigh up whether he was telling the truth. "You mean like dog food?"

He smiled. "Something like that."

He turned to the couch, where her mother was slouched, watching the show.

"I still prefer the sixties Batman with Adam West," she grumbled. "Biff, bang, kapow!"

He rolled his eyes. "No one appreciates great TV when it's animated."

"I had no idea you were such a nerd."

He sat down, grimacing as his hip emitted a few mild tremors of pain. "So are you enjoying your trip to London so far?"

He had directed the question at Mason, but Holly answered instead. "Yes! I want to go on the London Eye again. Are we really going to move, Mummy? Can we please move here so I can go on it every day?"

Mason caught his eye briefly as she answered.

"We'll see, sweetie. We'll see."

Epilogue

She awoke as though from a long hibernation, feeling like she had been asleep for months. But it took only a few seconds before the memories rushed back into her brain, like water surging through a hole into a damaged vessel.

How damaged, Lucy?

She remembered the cavern, the savage blow Bram – Donald – had struck her. The vicious horror of Hardacre's dog as he had attacked them. The pain of his teeth sinking into her face. She instinctively tried to reach upwards, to touch her damaged flesh, but found that her hands wouldn't move.

She was sitting on something firm but comfortable, perhaps a padded chair. Her arms were tied behind her back and her feet bound together at the ankles. There was some sort of cloth sack or hood over her head, but she could make out light through the fabric, and a shape moving about, to her right.

"What… what's going on?" she mumbled, trying to sound firm but instead sounding quiet and fearful. Her mouth felt numb and swollen.

"Ah!" came a sprightly response. "Glad you're finally back with us. I was worried I'd gone overboard with the sedatives."

That voice…

"Sedatives? What… happened to me?"

She remembered escaping into the tunnels, fleeing madly, in no particular direction. Desperate to escape from the bloodshed, the chaos. To survive.

"Oh, Lucy… don't you worry about that for now. Soon you won't need to ask any questions at all."

The silhouetted shape loomed large over her, and she shrank back in her seat.

"Shhh," the voice said in a soothing tone, as the hood was snatched away from her head. The light in the room was dim, but still it made her squint, as if she had spent weeks in total darkness.

She was in a small workshop of some kind. Around her were shelves, stacked boxes, and a couple of workbenches littered with tools and thick reference books. The door had to be behind her, and there were no windows – the light came from a single light bulb hanging from the ceiling. The place smelt musty and damp.

As her vision adjusted, she looked up at the man standing next to her, the man with the familiar voice.

"Bill? What… what am I doing here? Why am I tied up?"

Bill Cronin smiled down at her, his expression full of sympathy and regret; the same look a parent might give a child that was about to undergo an unpleasant dental operation. He didn't reply, and instead reached out to place a hand on her forehead, his fingers feeling dry and papery as he smoothed her hair into place.

Then he moved behind her, disappearing from view.

It was only when she was suddenly tipped backwards and spun around that she realised she was sitting in a wheelchair. Cronin pushed her through an open door that led into a long, dark corridor. She wriggled and thrashed, but her bonds held tight. Cronin didn't seem to notice as he continued to propel her forwards.

"Would you believe it's been two weeks? I hope you don't mind me keeping you unconscious while I worked. I'd have enjoyed your company… but I knew you wouldn't *sit still*."

The passageway led to another door, this one hanging ajar. Cronin used the wheelchair to bump it open, pushing her into a larger chamber. This one wasn't filled with boxes and tools. It was a living room, complete with fireplace, sofa, TV set.

And corpses, arranged all around her.

One of them was nailed to the wall, directly opposite, positioned in an upside-down cross. It had no skin. Others were sitting on the couch, their limbs jutting out at impossible angles, crude stitching showing where the appendages had been removed, swapped, sewn back into place. One woman, lying on the ground at her feet, should have been face down… but her head had been reattached the wrong way, so instead she stared up at Lucy, her preserved features contorted into a repulsive smile.

Lucy didn't have the energy to scream. All that came out of her was a strangled sob. What was this place? What was going on?

"Ta-da!" exclaimed Cronin as he strode back out in front of her. "What do you think?"

Lucy felt her breathing quicken as bile rose in her throat. She tried to look away from the atrocities, but the bodies seemed to be everywhere she turned. All women. All blonde. All mutilated.

"Speechless eh? I'm not surprised. It's taken me an awfully long time to get this into a fit state to share with the public. You wouldn't believe how many evenings I've slaved away in here, trying to get the expressions just right…" He caressed the cheek of one of the cadavers, and Lucy shuddered, horrified. "Anyway," he continued, cheerily. "It's time for the *pièce de résistance*!"

He walked towards the curtains, which were drawn back to reveal the large living room windows. These were fake, the white frames stuck onto a painted black wall; there was no natural light, as though they were underground. Lucy realised with a start that the room was a replica of Leonard Spitt's living room at Smalley Street, perhaps exactly as it had been found by Donald, all those years earlier. She had never seen the room, but she knew all about what had happened, what Leonard had done with the bodies of their sacrifices.

Cronin reached behind the curtain and began to pull another figure from behind it. "She's shy, bless her. And I understand why; this is her debut, after all!"

Lucy tried to avert her eyes, not wanting to see what new nightmare was about to be unveiled. But she couldn't tear her gaze away. She watched as a bare arm emerged, followed by a slender body wearing a black cocktail dress.

She gaped. Her breath froze on her lips. In her veins, her blood was like ice water.

She was staring into her own face.

"We were born on the *same day*, would you believe? Me and him, I mean. It's no surprise I've always felt a connection." Cronin was staring into the eyes of the doppelgänger as he spoke. "He was a great artist. When I found his marvellous work in the tunnels, I suppose I felt… compelled to continue his legacy. It's been lovely and peaceful down there, all these years. And then suddenly, this week… it's been like a *madhouse*."

They weren't real bodies… everything here was an effigy, a representation of what had happened, eighteen years earlier.

"Bill… I'm sorry… I'm sorry for what we did. I was trying to put it right… I'll go to the police. I'll confess."

Cronin turned to look at her, tilting his head quizzically. "I don't know who Bill is, Lucy. My name is Doctor Mephisto."

She groaned and started to struggle once again.

"It's very good of him, to let me keep you," her captor continued, turning to address his waxwork creation once again. "He really has no reason to allow me even this small mercy."

She felt the bonds yield, just slightly.

"The last girl he asked for managed to escape and cause a great deal of fuss. I suppose I'm getting old, and sloppy…" He sighed sadly. "It's a good job I found that writer, wandering the tunnels. It's not an easy thing you know, faking someone's suicide, but I think I managed to tie everything up quite neatly."

"You mean… the writer *wasn't* the copycat?"

"Copycat…" Cronin repeated, still gazing lovingly into the eyes of the disturbingly lifelike Lucy Chen simulacrum. "I don't think you quite understand."

He turned suddenly, walking past her, back out into the corridor. She was left alone in that terrible room of death. Death that she had caused, had condoned, had celebrated, along with her lover, Thomas Hardacre. She had been so young, so easily led. And he hadn't cared about her deformity, hadn't even mentioned it. He had called her beautiful. Not 'freak' or 'monster' or 'octopus'.

She tugged again at her bonds, feeling them slacken some more. A few more minutes and she might be free… but then she heard Cronin re-enter the room behind her and stopped struggling. He stood at her side, staring down at her wordlessly. After a while, she dared to glance up at him.

This time, she did scream.

It wasn't Cronin. She was looking up into the awful, empty smile of Leonard Spitt. She strained and tore at her bonds, almost pulling the chair onto its side in her efforts to get away from this ghost, this reanimated horror. The worst part was his *eyes* – gazing down at her, through her, not gazing at all, two staring orbs as lifeless as marbles.

She screamed again. She couldn't help it. She screamed loud and long, shaking the chair from side to side, feeling the knots around her wrists almost coming undone.

Calmly, Spitt produced a long syringe from the pocket of his coat, and moved it towards her. In sheer panic, she tried to bite his hand, but despite her resistance he managed to slide the needle into her flesh of her upper arm.

It took only seconds for her limbs to feel leaden, her eyelids to begin to droop. The bonds finally broke and fell away from her hands, but she could no longer move them.

The last thing she saw before unconsciousness claimed her was her vision blurring as Spitt slipped a plastic bag over her head. The last thing she felt was a cord tightening around her throat. The last thing she heard was a soft hissing sound.

She breathed in, tasting nothing, smelling nothing, and drifted into oblivion.

He waited until he was sure she was dead, then removed the bag, and turned off the nitrogen canister. He wheeled her body back into the passageway, taking a different turn, the wheelchair clattering as it bumped down a few stairs towards a different room. He didn't care about the noise. They were deep beneath the museum, alone, safe within his kingdom.

He lingered over her for a few moments, admiring the job he had done of dyeing her hair. Blonde, just like Leonard wanted. Personally, he really did prefer her as he had captured her in wax: raven-haired and dazzling, as she had been in life, ignoring her terrible, fresh facial scars.

What a waste.

But it didn't matter what he thought. His desires, his needs, were irrelevant.

He was merely a vessel

Cronin took off the rubber mask, and wheeled Lucy Chen towards the blue barrels in the corner of the storage room. The police had taken Leonard's bones from him, so he wasn't yet sure how he would be able to convey her spirit to his master. But one step at a time. First, he needed to melt her down, and that would take quite a while.